Dying for an answer . . .

"*You* did this to me, Jessica! Why?" Bruce yelled, shaking her hard, his voice growing louder and more hysterical with every word. "What kind of poison was it?"

"*Poison!*" Jessica exclaimed. "You're delirious! I don't even know what you're talking about."

Bruce shook her so roughly that her head snapped back and forth. "I'm not kidding, Jessica—what's the antidote?"

"I don't know!"

"The antidote, Jessica!" Bruce screamed, forcing her back against the wall.

Jessica let out a strangled cry as her head hit the wall, her back and shoulders pinned tightly. Her heart hammered at her rib cage, and her breaths were short and harsh with fear. "Stop it!" she yelled, slapping him across the face with all her strength. "Let go of me right *now!*"

The blow raised an angry red patch on the sallow skin of his cheek. Then, very slowly, he released her shoulders and backed away, shaking his head as if confused.

"What's going on here, Bruce?" Jessica demanded, sensing she'd gained the upper hand. "Are you still sick?"

"I'm dying."

SWEET VALLEY UNIVERSITY®

THRILLER EDITION

Dead Before Dawn

Written by
Laurie John

Created by
FRANCINE PASCAL

BANTAM BOOKS
NEW YORK · TORONTO · LONDON · SYDNEY · AUCKLAND

SWEET VALLEY UNIVERSITY THRILLER:
DEAD BEFORE DAWN
A BANTAM BOOK : 0 553 50640 4

Originally published in USA by Bantam Books

First publication in Great Britain

PRINTING HISTORY
Bantam edition published 1997

Conceived by Francine Pascal

Produced by Daniel Weiss Associates, Inc,
33 West 17th Street, New York, NY 10011

Bantam Books are published by Transworld Publishers Ltd,
61–63 Uxbridge Road, Ealing, London W5 5SA,
in Australia by Transworld Publishers (Australia) Pty Ltd,
15–25 Helles Avenue, Moorebank, NSW 2170,
and in New Zealand by Transworld Publishers (NZ) Ltd,
3 William Pickering Drive, Albany, Auckland.

Printed and bound in Great Britain by
Cox & Wyman Ltd, Reading, Berkshire.

To Edy Rees

Chapter One

The mysterious poison has completed its work. Choking and gasping, the victim falls to the floor, dead. He'll never know who took his life. Or why. . . .

Bruce Patman leaned back in his leather desk chair, surveying the words on the glowing monitor in front of him with complete satisfaction.

"It's perfect," he said aloud, savoring the moment. Bruce had poured every ounce of himself into this screenwriting assignment for Professor Gordon's class, and now . . . it was finished. *Finally.* With a sigh Bruce tore his eyes away from the computer screen and glanced around his apartment, taking in the old pizza boxes and mountains of discarded, crumpled papers. "It *ought* to be perfect," he added ruefully. He'd barely even left his apartment during the last two weeks, and now yet another weekend had flown by, practically unnoticed.

Bruce rose from his chair stiffly and headed over to the window, stretching in his wrinkled T-shirt and silk boxers.

The dawn of an early Monday was spreading across Sweet Valley and streaming through his unclosed blinds. He watched, half dazed from lack of sleep, as the sky gradually lightened, illuminating the street outside his off-campus apartment. *Another all-nighter,* he said to himself in amazement. *That makes two in a row. I never thought a guy could be so tired and still manage to stay awake.*

"And all for a school assignment!" he exclaimed with a snort of ironic laughter. "If my friends could see me now, they wouldn't believe it!"

It wasn't only because of his unshowered, half-clothed, and uncharacteristically grungy appearance, but also for his sudden attention to homework. Bruce wasn't exactly famous for his seriousness as a student, but since he'd hooked up with Professor Gordon, all that had changed.

Dennis Gordon was a Sweet Valley University professor whose Academy Award–winning script for *Night Falls Slowly* had made him a household name. Bruce could barely believe his good luck when he'd been accepted into Professor Gordon's prestigious screenwriting class, one of SVU's most sought-after courses.

"I'd better get this thing printed out," he

2

muttered, hurrying back to the computer. Bruce hit a few keys to make two copies of his screenplay—one for his professor and one for himself—before wandering off toward the bathroom. He turned on the water in the sink and splashed his face a few times, dimly aware of the rhythmic hum of the laser printer in the living room. When he raised his head to grab a towel off the bar, he caught a glimpse of his reflection and gasped.

"You look like hell, Patman!" he exclaimed in surprise before rubbing his face vigorously with one of his monogrammed towels. After two weeks of living like a starving artist, Bruce hadn't expected his appearance to be up to his usual high standards, but the sight that met his eyes appalled him. His usually intense blue eyes were bloodshot beneath his heavy brows, he had a two-week growth of dark beard, and his skin was as pale as if he'd been living under a rock. Not only that but his brown hair stuck out all over as if it hadn't been combed in weeks. Bruce winced at the thought of what his girlfriend, Lila Fowler, would say if she caught him looking so repulsive.

"Oh *no!* Lila!" Bruce groaned, slapping his forehead. "This time she's going to kill me."

Lila had called the night before, right when he was in the middle of writing the most exciting scene of the entire screenplay. "I haven't seen

3

you in two weeks, Bruce," she'd complained. "You don't *really* expect me to believe that you've been working on one thing this whole time."

The clock is ticking . . . the victim is getting sicker . . . his time is running out. . . .

"I'll call you back in ten minutes," Bruce had promised, hanging up. He never had.

"Well, that's it. I'm dead," he told himself, walking back into the living room. Lila could be understanding when she wanted to be, but Bruce had a feeling that this wasn't going to be one of those times. In the last two weeks he'd begged out of two standing dates and refused to take her to a spur-of-the-moment sorority dance. Each time she'd been a little less thrilled with him. Now he'd blown her off over the phone; there was no worse move than that, especially where Lila was concerned.

Bruce groaned and reached for the growing stack of paper on his printer, flipping it faceup. *The Victim,* proclaimed the first page in large, bold letters. Then, in slightly smaller print, *by Bruce Patman.* He had to admit it looked good. It looked *very* good.

And that's just the title page, he congratulated himself. *Wait till Professor Gordon reads that opening scene!* In spite of his exhaustion and the major apologizing he saw in his future, Bruce found himself becoming excited again.

He'd never worked so hard on anything in his life as he had on this screenplay—let alone on something for school! And it was good too. Maybe *really* good. This wasn't the kind of script that would get turned in for a grade and then be forgotten. No, Bruce dared to think he could actually sell it and see it be made into a movie.

"That would be so unbelievable," he day-dreamed out loud as the second copy of his masterpiece began pouring out of the printer. Bruce imagined himself walking down the red carpet at the Academy Awards with Lila on his arm while the screaming fans behind the barricades went crazy. She'd be wearing something hot and slinky, of course, and his new tuxedo would be perfect—it ought to be, since every top menswear designer in the world would have sent him something custom-made and practically begged him for the honor of wearing it.

"I'd like to thank the Academy for this great honor," Bruce announced impulsively, grabbing up a black marking pen to serve as his microphone. "And Dennis Gordon, my mentor, a man who knows raw talent when he sees it. And . . . and myself, of course. After all, none of this could have happened without me!" The imagined crowd went crazy, loving him for all he was worth. "And most of all," Bruce continued, loading his voice with Hollywood sincerity, "I'd like

5

to thank my beautiful girlfriend—no—my *fi-ancée*, Lila Fowler." He closed his eyes and saw Lila walking up the broad stairs to join him at the microphone, an enormous diamond engagement ring flashing on her hand. "Ladies and gentlemen of the Academy, allow me to introduce my future wife."

Assuming, of course, that Lila would be speaking to me again by then, he thought with a grimace as cold reality intruded on his fantasy. There was no getting around it. He had some *serious* kissing up to do.

Suddenly the printer stopped humming, and an error box came up on his computer screen. The printer was out of paper, with half of the second copy to go. Cursing, Bruce yanked open the desk drawer where he kept the extra paper, only to find it empty. "Great!" he muttered. "*Now* what am I supposed to do?" He began a frantic search through the other drawers, finally locating a thick stack of pink paper left over from the days when he'd printed up flyers for Lila's Doughnuts, the not-for-profit doughnut shop that had been a disaster to run but a windfall to sell.

"It *had* to be pink," he grumbled, stuffing the leftover paper into the printer. It was annoying, but it didn't really matter. He already had one good plain copy to turn in to Professor Gordon; he could keep this half-pink one for himself.

The second copy finished printing and Bruce lifted it off the printer, fastening it with a heavy clip. The pink paper reminded him of Lila, filling him first with dread, then inspiration.

Hey, I know! I'll print a copy for Li too, Bruce decided suddenly. *That way she'll see how hard I've been working.* Under the circumstances, it seemed like a good idea. Who knew? Maybe Lila would even be impressed enough with the screenplay to forgive him.

Then Bruce had an even better idea. Dropping back into his desk chair, he hammered out a few new lines on the keyboard. A second later the printer began printing an all-pink copy of the screenplay, incorporating the new page he'd just written. He smiled, satisfied. "That won't get me completely out of the doghouse," he said aloud, his eyes still on the monitor. "But it's a start."

"I'm telling you, Isabella," Lila complained. "The way Bruce has been acting lately just isn't normal. I think his body's been invaded by aliens or something."

"Such a shame," Isabella Ricci teased, her gray eyes sparkling. "But you have to give those aliens credit. They sure picked a great body!"

The two Theta Alpha Theta sorority sisters were sitting on a grassy rise at the edge of the quad, tanning their legs during a break between Monday classes.

"I'm not kidding!" Lila protested, throwing a blade of grass at Isabella. "Well, not much anyway," she added grudgingly. "Seriously, Izzy, can you remember Bruce *ever* spending this kind of time on his homework before? It's unnatural."

"Well, it is kind of *unusual*," Isabella allowed.

"No. Un*natural*," Lila repeated emphatically. "I haven't seen him for *two weeks*. Last night I called him up, thinking maybe we could get together, and do you know what he told me?"

"I have no idea."

"He said he couldn't talk, but he'd call me back in ten minutes."

Isabella shrugged. "That's not so horrible."

"No? How about if I told you he never called me back?" Lila could tell she'd finally made her point. Shock registered on Isabella's pretty face.

"Uh-oh," she said. "*That's* pretty horrible."

"You're not kidding," Lila grumbled. "He's in deep trouble."

"Heads up!" a male voice called suddenly from across the lawn. Lila and Isabella recoiled instinctively with barely enough time to miss being clobbered by a competition black Frisbee. It whizzed past their faces and dive-bombed into the grass a few feet away.

"What kind of idiot—" Lila began angrily, turning in the direction from which the Frisbee had sailed. Her eyes widened abruptly, and she bit off her words in midsentence. The idiot in question was heading their way—and he was *gorgeous!*

"Wow, I'm so sorry," he apologized, smiling sheepishly as he bent to retrieve the Frisbee. "I'm usually a little more coordinated."

I'll bet you are, Lila couldn't help thinking as she looked him over. He was very tall—maybe six-foot five—with thick, wavy blond hair and magnetic brown eyes. His smile showed off straight, perfect white teeth.

Lila let her gaze drop from his face down over his T-shirt and white shorts to his well-muscled legs. Her eyes snapped back up to the T-shirt in a flash. When Lila read Hillhaven Preparatory Academy, emblazoned above an ornate, old-fashioned school seal, an involuntary smile flitted across her face. Hillhaven Prep was one of the most expensive and exclusive boarding schools in the country. *So he's not only good-looking but wealthy and well-bred too,* Lila thought, wetting her lips. *Who is this guy?*

"I'm Marcus Stanton," he introduced himself, right on cue. "I'm really sorry about that, um . . ."

"Lila. Lila Fowler," she finished for him. She accepted the hand he offered and shook it delicately, noticing that the sunglasses perched atop his head were pricey Optimax originals. "And this is my friend Isabella."

Marcus smiled at Isabella, but Lila couldn't help seeing how eagerly he turned his attention back to her. She sat up straighter on the lawn, adjusting her white sundress over her knees and shading her eyes with one perfectly manicured hand.

"Did you go to Hillhaven?" she asked, pointing to his T-shirt.

"Yes." His smile broadened. "Do you know it?"

Did she know it? Did she have the floor plan of every store on Rodeo Drive committed to memory? "Of *course*. I have a few friends who went there," Lila allowed, trying not to sound too interested. "But you look like you may have been a grade or two ahead of them."

"Hey, Marcus!" yelled an impatient voice from across the lawn. "What are you doing? Come on!"

Marcus turned and flung the Frisbee in the direction of the voice, then dropped cross-legged on the ground in front of Lila. "Like who?" he asked.

"Shelly Mitchell," Lila said, naming the first person she thought of. "We used to go to camp together."

"What a coincidence!" Marcus exclaimed. "Sure, I know Shelly. How is she?"

Lila hadn't actually seen Shelly for years, but she didn't want to admit it right then. "Fine," she lied, searching for a way out. Instantly she noticed that Marcus's shorts were regulation tennis whites and that his tan stopped at the ankles. "So, were you on the Hillhaven tennis team?"

10

"Varsity squad; you bet," Marcus replied. "Do you play?"

"When I feel like it."

"We should play together sometime," Marcus offered. He faked a backhanded volley, and the sunlight glinted off the heavy gold ID bracelet on his wrist. "Do you belong to the country club?"

"Who doesn't?"

"Come *on*, Marcus," his Frisbee partner yelled again. "I thought you wanted to play."

"I do," Marcus told Lila with a wink. "Just not with him." The flirtatious glint in his deep brown eyes left Lila speechless, her cheeks flushing.

"I'll call you," he added, rising to his feet. "What's your phone number?"

"You don't really expect me to tell you that," Lila answered, smiling coyly.

Marcus shrugged. "I'm a resourceful guy. I'll find it myself." He lowered his sunglasses over his eyes and flashed her a devastatingly handsome grin before he went to rejoin his friend.

"Wow," Isabella breathed as soon as Marcus was out of earshot. "That guy's a serious fox."

"Izzy!" Lila protested. "What are you doing, looking at other guys? What would Danny say?"

Isabella seemed unconcerned about the reaction of her steady boyfriend, Danny Wyatt, as she lifted her dark hair off her bare shoulders, swishing it back and forth to cool herself. "I don't know, Li. What would *Bruce* say?"

What would *Bruce say?* Lila wondered with a twinge of guilt. But she quickly stuffed down the emotion. "Who cares?" she said breezily. "The way he's been acting lately, Bruce is lucky I haven't eloped with the ice-cream man."

Isabella laughed. "The ice-cream man couldn't afford you."

"Maybe not," Lila agreed, her eyes on a distant Marcus Stanton. "But I've suddenly remembered something very important."

"What's that?"

A slow, mischievous smile crossed Lila's face. "Bruce Patman isn't the only gorgeous rich boy in the world."

It was after one o'clock when Bruce parked his black Porsche at the curb in front of Lila's off-campus apartment complex. He'd have to hurry if he was going to be on time for his two o'clock screenwriting class, but he desperately wanted to make up with Lila first.

When Bruce got out of the car, he bent to check his reflection in the window, smiling at what he saw. A few hours of resting in the sun had been followed by a shave, a shower, and a trip to his stylist for a trim. She had been booked solid when he'd called for an appointment, but he'd schmoozed her good and she'd found a way to wedge him in.

"The old Patman charm," he told himself,

12

flicking some lint off the collar of his denim-blue, raw silk shirt. The shirt brought out the color of his eyes, which were almost back to normal now that the Visine had taken effect. All and all he was back to his usual, incomparable self. Fully satisfied, Bruce squared his broad shoulders, brushed the seat of his black jeans, and prepared to sweep Lila off her feet.

I hope she's home, he thought, digging through his backpack. He retrieved the pink copy of *The Victim,* the one he'd printed just for her, then locked the pack in the car. He'd been calling Lila on and off all day, but the only thing picking up her phone had been her answering machine. Given the current circumstances, leaving a message didn't seem like such a good idea.

Bruce strode up the walk to Lila's apartment, his custom black cowboy boots loud against the red-brick paving. The apartment complex was old and beautiful, with six individual cottages arranged around a central grassy courtyard. Each Spanish-style unit had its own ornately carved front door with a tiny, private porch. Bruce reached Lila's apartment at the back of the complex just in time to see a good-looking guy setting down an enormous bouquet of roses on Lila's front porch.

"Hey! What do you think you're doing?" Bruce demanded loudly and indignantly.

The man jerked upright and spun around. "Jeez!" he exclaimed. "You scared me."

"Who told you you could bring my girlfriend flowers?" Bruce growled jealously. "Who do you think you are?"

The guy on the doorstep held up his hands in a gesture of peace, and for the first time Bruce noticed the clipboard in his hand. "Don't shoot *me*, buddy," he pleaded good-naturedly. "I'm just the messenger." He pointed to the florist's logo on the left breast of his green polo shirt. "See? I'm only delivering them."

"Sorry," Bruce murmured, feeling a little foolish. Of *course* Lila wasn't getting flowers from some other guy—she could never be *that* mad at him. "Who are they from, then?"

The flower guy shrugged. "That's not my department. Listen, she's not home. You want to sign for these?"

Bruce took the clipboard and signed where the flower guy pointed, all the while wondering who had sent his girlfriend roses—and *red* roses at that. *They'd better be from her parents*, he thought possessively, *or there's going to be hell to pay.*

"Thanks, man." The flower guy took back the clipboard, tucked it under his arm, and headed down the walkway toward the street. Bruce waited until he climbed into his van and drove away before bending over, snatching the

14

card from the roses, and quickly reading the note inside.

Dear Lila,

    I *told* you I'd find you. I'm sorry for almost hitting you with the Frisbee today. If I'd known I'd meet such a beautiful woman that way, I'd have taken up the sport a long time ago. I'd love to take you to dinner sometime. Call me.

Marcus
555-6689

Bruce stared at the card in disbelief. The flowers *were* from a guy! Didn't anyone tell this jerk that Lila already had a boyfriend?

Didn't *Lila* tell him?

Bruce's chest grew tight with jealous anger. Someone had some serious explaining to do, and it wasn't him.

"Lila!" he shouted furiously, pounding on her door. "Open up! *Lila!*" But as the flower guy had already warned him, Lila wasn't home.

How could Lila do this to me? Bruce fumed, trying to decide what to do. *And especially today, when we should be celebrating the completion of my first screenplay?*

Angrily Bruce stuffed Marcus's card into his shirt pocket. Then he removed the little plastic cardholder from the bouquet and flung it into the neighbor's bushes. After dropping his screenplay directly in front of Lila's door, Bruce lifted the heavy vase of roses and set it right on top of the thick, pink stack of paper.

"That'll teach him," Bruce muttered as he walked stiffly back to his car. "And if I ever catch that miserable, sneaking dirtbag anywhere *near* Lila, he's a dead man."

Chapter Two

Now I'm late on top of everything else, Bruce thought angrily as he hurried down the outside aisle of the film center. *I've never been late for Professor Gordon's screenwriting class before. I hope I didn't miss anything good.* The only open seats were in the very front row, and Bruce had to walk in front of the entire class to get to one. He slid into an empty chair, still steaming.

If he didn't find out what was going on between Lila and that Marcus jerk soon, it was going to drive him crazy. Professor Gordon's lecture, usually the high point of Bruce's Monday, was registering as nothing more than a hum in the back of his mind. The sound of his own blood boiling was all he heard as he mentally read and reread Marcus's pathetic little love note.

In his heart, of course, Bruce knew Marcus was really just wasting his time. After all, Bruce

17

and Lila were deeply in love. Lila would never leave him for someone else. Would she?

No, of course not! he shouted inwardly. But then again, Lila *was* awfully mad at him. . . . Suddenly Bruce's fury gave way to apprehension and a hollow, prickling sensation in his gut. *Don't think about it anymore,* he told himself. *Snap out of it and listen to the lecture.*

"As you all know," Professor Gordon's voice resounded, "your screenplays are due today. You may turn them in after class, but I'll be in my office until five o'clock if you'd rather bring yours there. I'm looking forward to reading some brilliant work!"

At the mention of brilliant work Bruce unconsciously sat up a little straighter in his front-row seat, the excitement he'd felt earlier in the day rushing back to him. *Forget about the flowers,* he told himself, forcing the subject out of his mind. *Just make sure you hand in that screenplay. Then you'll catch up with Lila tonight and get this whole mess straightened out.*

Once that was taken care of, how would he manage to sit and wait patiently for Professor Gordon's opinion of his script? *I'll go by his office and drop it off personally,* Bruce decided. *If I butter him up, maybe he'll read mine first.*

"So you see that the screenwriter's primary obligation is to *story* and to the dialogue and actions that will advance that story," Professor Gordon concluded his lecture. "It is not the writer's job to specify every camera angle in minute detail, to tell the actors exactly what kind of expression and tone of voice they should use for each utterance, or—God forbid—to fill the margins with endless ideas regarding casting and wardrobe. The writer must stay focused on the story."

Jessica Wakefield's pen scribbled frantically as she tried to write down every word. Professor Gordon's screenwriting class was hands down the best class she'd taken in all her thirteen years in school—fourteen if you counted kindergarten. Bruce Patman had actually given her some decent advice for once.

Jessica glanced up from her notebook toward the front row of the classroom, where she could see the back of Bruce's head. She'd seen him come in late, looking totally teed off.

I wonder if Lila finally caught up with him, Jessica thought, amused. Everyone with ears knew how angry her best friend was about Bruce's recent neglect. *Boy, would I have liked to have seen* that!

"Before we finish up for today," Professor Gordon boomed, "I want to remind everyone that the new Beringer Wing of the film school is going to be dedicated on Thursday afternoon, and I would like all of you to attend the dedication ceremony. You all received the flyers I passed out last week or, if you lost yours, you can copy the information off one of the posters." Professor Gordon gestured distractedly in the direction of the hallway, which Jessica knew was wallpapered with posters announcing the event.

A serious-looking girl seated next to Jessica leaned over and whispered, "Are you going?"

"Are you kidding?" Jessica whispered back. "I wouldn't miss it for anything." Practically everyone on campus knew the tragic story of Belinda Beringer, the teen suicide who'd had everything and thrown it all away. But Jessica had become *obsessed* with it.

Belinda's wealthy, high-profile family had put a lot of pressure on her to excel, and on the surface she seemed to have been handling it brilliantly. She had been the top student in the SVU film department a couple of years back, and her professors had predicted that she was going to make it big. On top of all that she was amazingly beautiful—with dark, silky hair and striking, amber-colored eyes. But to everyone's amazement, Belinda had been found dead in her dorm room of an overdose, with no money left in her enormous trust fund.

Jessica remembered how the media had had a field day with Belinda's story, reporting on how she'd torn up all her schoolwork and left nothing behind but some scribbled class notes. The media suggested that Belinda had blown her trust fund on drugs and killed herself when she felt she couldn't live up to all those expectations, but everyone who knew her denied it vehemently. The entire population of Sweet Valley had been shocked. Belinda had barely been nineteen.

I know—my next screenplay will be Belinda Beringer's life story, Jessica vowed, suddenly inspired. It was perfect: a rich, beautiful heroine; an early, tragic, mysterious death. *I can practically see it already. . . .*

"Well, that's everything," Professor Gordon announced, breaking through Jessica's reverie. "I'll look for you all on Thursday."

Her classmates surged to their feet amid a loud rustling of books and papers. But Jessica took her time, slipping her notebook into her backpack and slowly taking out an expensively bound copy of *Night Falls Slowly*, Professor Gordon's Academy Award–winning screenplay. She ran her hand over the maroon cover nervously, waiting for her fellow students to deposit their screenplays on the table up front and leave the room. After a few minutes the room had cleared enough for Jessica to confidently approach the professor.

"Professor Gordon? Uh, I was wondering," she began awkwardly. "Um . . . that is, if it's not too much trouble . . . would you please autograph this copy of your script for my sister, Elizabeth?" Jessica clumsily thrust the leather-bound screenplay toward the professor and held it at arm's length.

Professor Gordon's green eyes lit with interest. "That's a limited edition." He took the screenplay and turned it over in his hands, examining the binding. "I don't mean to brag, but this is worth a lot of money now. Is it yours?"

"Er, no," Jessica admitted reluctantly. "It's my sister's." She had no intention of adding that when Elizabeth had laid out her hard-earned allowance for the screenplay, Jessica had made fun of her. In fact, Jessica hadn't even known who Dennis Gordon was back then. And she certainly wasn't about to go into how her twin sister had reacted when only Jessica had been able to squeak into his screenwriting course after they'd both applied for it.

"Your sister must be a woman of discriminating tastes," Professor Gordon said, reaching for the fountain pen in his jacket pocket. A touch of a smile played around the corners of his handsome mouth. His curly black hair was thick and just slightly out of control, and the deeply etched laugh lines at the corners of his green eyes stood out pale against his dark tan. Maybe she hadn't known that her professor was famous, but no one needed to point out to her that he was also completely gorgeous.

"I'm discriminating too," Jessica blurted. "Elizabeth is my identical twin. I mean, we *look* identical, but we're really completely different. Well, we're not *completely* different, but we're not very alike either. We're both very discriminating, though."

Jessica knew she was babbling, but she was so overawed to be having a private conversation with the formidable Dennis Gordon that she couldn't seem to stop herself.

"How would you like me to sign it?" he asked, his pen poised over the title page.

"What? Oh, uh, I don't know." *Why hadn't I thought about that before?* she chastised herself. "Just 'To Elizabeth,' I guess."

Professor Gordon smiled more strongly, making the corners of his eyes crinkle adorably. "Well, maybe I can come up with something a *little* more personal," he said, pausing a moment before he began to write. Jessica read over his shoulder as the gold nib of his fountain pen filled the page with swift, bold strokes.

> To Elizabeth—a lovely young woman, judging from the mirror image in front of me. See you at the movies!
> Dennis Gordon

"How's that?" he asked, handing the open script back to Jessica. The still-wet blue ink glistened under the fluorescent lights.

"Wow," she breathed like a starstruck fan,

blushing as she realized how terribly unsophisticated she'd sounded. "I mean, it's very nice," she amended in her most adult voice. "Thank you."

Professor Gordon began gathering up his things. "No problem. Now, don't you have something for me too?"

"Do I?" Jessica asked, startled.

"I believe there's the little matter of a homework assignment." He held out his hand expectantly. "Your script? You *did* write one, didn't you?"

"Oh! Yes!" Jessica exclaimed. She'd been so focused on getting his signature that she'd totally forgotten to hand in her own screenplay. She set the open copy of *Night Falls Slowly* carefully on the table, then rummaged through her backpack for the thin folder that contained her movie script. "It's in sort of . . . *rough* shape at the moment," she apologized, handing it to Professor Gordon. "I, uh, I kind of wish I'd heard today's lecture before I wrote it."

"How so?" he asked, taking the folder from her hand and dropping it into his open briefcase.

"Well . . . ," she began haltingly. "You might find one or two notes in the margins about what I thought the characters should be wearing. Sorry."

Professor Gordon laughed. "I won't hold that against you this time," he promised, his green eyes sparkling.

Jessica smiled weakly. Actually, now that she

thought about it, she'd noted *exactly* what she thought every single character should be wearing in every single scene. She just hadn't really noted what they were supposed to be *doing*. *Why couldn't I have thought of the Belinda Beringer idea* earlier? She groaned silently.

"My next script will be better," she offered, feeling as if she had to make some kind of positive impression on him before he read the disaster she'd just turned in. She never should have listened when Lila told her to write about models vacationing in Paris! "I came up with a great story idea during class today. It's all about this beautiful, talented woman who commits suicide."

"Hmmm," the professor said dryly. "I wonder what made you think of that."

Jessica blushed a deeper crimson. *Great. Now he thinks I'm a plagiarist too.* "So when will the world see *your* next script?" she asked brightly, eager to change the subject. "It's been a while since *Night Falls Slowly* came out."

"*Don't* remind me," Professor Gordon drawled, slamming his briefcase shut and getting up from the table. "It's a hard act to follow, and no one knows that better than I do."

"What's it going to be about?" Jessica asked, unable to stop herself. "Will it be a sequel, or are you trying something new?"

Professor Gordon looked at his watch and waved her off. "Look, I'm late for office hours," he said. "Some other time, OK?" Then without another word he swung his briefcase off the table and strode quickly from the room.

Oh no, Jessica cried internally as Professor Gordon's tall frame disappeared down the hallway. *What did I do to make him run off like that? Was I babbling too much?*

Jessica ran back over the conversation in her mind. *I never should have mentioned Belinda,* she realized. After all, Belinda had been Professor Gordon's star student. *Why did I have to be so totally insensitive?*

"Great," she muttered, her voice sounding hollow in the emptiness of the film center. "There goes my grade." At the thought of grades Jessica remembered her screenplay and groaned out loud. "And what will he think of me after he reads *Supermodel Shop-a-thon?*"

Lila let herself into her apartment, her arms loaded down with Bruce's screenplay and an enormous vase of roses. "Pink paper. How weird," she remarked, dumping them both on the coffee table in the living room before she went into the bedroom to get ready for a long, hot bath.

"It's going to take a lot more than flowers and a huge stack of pink paper, Bruce Patman," Lila muttered, completely unimpressed. "Especially today." Lila had spent the morning with a few of

26

her Theta sisters planning a charity breakfast for Valley House, a home for abandoned and abused children. It was a good thing she'd showed up too, because before she'd taken charge, they'd actually been planning to serve doughnuts. *Doughnuts!* Of course, the only acceptable choices were croissants and crepes. *They should have all dropped to their knees and thanked me for diverting such an abominable faux pas,* she thought briskly.

Lila had barely gotten the breakfast plans back on track when she'd had to leave to sit through a couple of classes, but it was just as well—she'd needed the rest. But after that she'd run into that interesting hunk Marcus playing Frisbee. Lila's brown eyes narrowed with pleasure at the memory. He was *so* nice, *so* gorgeous, and *so* cultivated. *Maybe I should have given him my phone number after all,* she thought, shaking her head to clear the idea. Still, the smile it had brought to her lips lingered.

As she massaged her shoulders Lila realized that it was the library that had truly worn her out. Because she tried to go there as seldom as possible, she had absolutely no idea where to find the books she needed for her literature assignment. *Why can't they just arrange the whole place alphabetically?* she wondered. *Then a person could go straight to L, for literature. Or T, for term paper. It's just that simple. Then there'd be no need for that stupid cataloging system!*

"An entire afternoon wasted," Lila said, kicking off her sandals and unbuttoning her sundress. When she noticed the red light on her answering machine blinking, she crossed the room and pushed the message button, her eyebrows arched expectantly.

"*Lila? This is Bruce. Are you there? Pick up the phone.*" Pause. "*OK. Uh . . . call you later. Bye.*" Beeep.

"*Li? Bruce again. Call me.*" Beeep.

"*Lila? Listen, I'm sorry about last night, OK? Call me as soon as you get home.*" Beeep.

"*Lila, where are you? Are you there? If you are, will you please pick up the phone?*" Pause. "*Hello?*" Slam! Beeep.

"*Come on, Lila . . .*"

Lila pushed the fast-forward button on the answering machine with a satisfied smirk. "I think I got the general idea," she purred. Maybe after she'd had a bubble bath she'd actually *look* at the flowers he'd bought her. If he did an especially good job of apologizing, she might even let him take her out to dinner.

Stepping out of her dress, Lila walked into the bathroom and began preparing her bath. When she reached out her hand to feel the water temperature, the telephone rang in the other room.

If that's Bruce, he can wait another hour, she

28

thought, turning off the water so she could hear the answering machine pick up.

"Lila? It's Isabella. Call me the *second* you get home. Alison has convinced Tina Chai that the menu for the Valley House breakfast is all wrong. The doughnuts are back, and now we're having sausages rolled up in pancakes and . . ."

Lila flew out of the bathroom, almost losing her footing on the slick tile floor. She vaulted across the bed and snatched up the receiver. "Hello? Izzy?"

"Lila!" Isabella exclaimed. "Am I glad you're home! You've *got* to get over here. Those heathens are changing all your plans."

"I'm on my way," Lila vowed. She hung up the phone, allowing herself only one reluctant glance in the direction of the bathroom. Her bath would have to wait. *Bruce* would have to wait. There was no way she was letting those twin witches Tina Chai and Alison Quinn destroy all her hard work.

Grabbing a clean sweater and pair of slacks from her closet, Lila dressed hurriedly, her mind on the impending battle. If Alison and Tina wanted a war, then that's exactly what they'd get!

"Nice try, Bruce," she quipped as she sped by the vase of red roses on her way out the door. "Maybe later."

Bruce hesitated in the hall outside the closed door of Professor Gordon's faculty office and nervously adjusted the straps of his backpack. He had wanted to wait until the last minute to drop off his screenplay so he could catch the professor alone, but dozens of latecomers had been streaming in and out of the office while Bruce stood in the hall. He didn't want to be interrupted once he got in the office, but five o'clock was rapidly approaching. If he held out any longer, his screenplay would be officially late.

"It's now or never," he said under his breath, rapping sharply on the office door.

"Come in," the professor's deep voice called.

Bruce turned the doorknob, pushed open the door, and stepped inside, his jaw dropping in amazement. Bruce certainly wasn't an expert on faculty offices, but the few he'd seen up to that point had been tiny, sterile cubicles. Professor Gordon's office, on the other hand, looked as though it had come straight out of the movies. It was huge, for one thing, but that was the least of it. The walls were paneled in a warm, dark wood. Built-in, floor-to-ceiling bookcases crammed with hundreds of books occupied the two end walls, while the wall across from the door contained a large window partially obscured by rich, burgundy draperies. The room seemed like something out of Harvard, or even Oxford, but not SVU.

"Cool!" Bruce breathed before he could stop himself and pretend to be unimpressed.

Professor Gordon laughed heartily and gestured Bruce toward two burgundy leather wing chairs facing his enormous mahogany desk. "I'm glad you approve. Have a seat, Mr. . . ."

"Patman." Bruce's feet sank into the thick oriental carpet as he crossed Professor Gordon's office and took the chair nearest the window. "Bruce Patman."

"Bruce . . . yes, of course."

"This is pretty nice for a faculty office," Bruce allowed, regaining his composure. He didn't want the professor to think he was some sort of unsophisticated schoolboy. After all, so what if the guy knew how to live a little? Bruce knew how to live high too. "I have to admit, you've got impeccable taste."

"Being a celebrity *does* have its advantages." Professor Gordon's smile was warm and slightly sardonic. "So what can I do for you?"

Before Bruce could answer, the professor abruptly pushed a pile of manuscripts on his desk to one side, upsetting a liquor decanter. Bruce caught it before it could fall, making sure nothing had spilled onto the leather-top desk.

"Whew!" exclaimed the professor, lifting the heavy crystal decanter from Bruce's hands and setting it carefully back on a corner of his desk. "Thanks for just saving my life! My mother gave me that when I won the Academy Award. I tried to tell her that professors in southern California don't make a habit of keeping Scotch in their offices, but she insisted." He shook his head and chuckled.

"Well, it sure goes with the rest of your office," Bruce followed up, wanting to show his professor that he was no amateur in the worldly sophistication department.

Professor Gordon looked around the room with obvious satisfaction. "Yes, it does, doesn't it? I always imagined I'd have an office like this someday. . . . I don't know why. It certainly didn't seem very likely when I was only a poor assistant professor, laboring in obscurity."

Bruce grinned and accepted his mentor's flair for melodrama. After all, he was an artist.

"So, then, let's get down to brass tacks," Professor Gordon quipped, interrupting his own musings. "I suppose you have a screenplay for me?"

"Yes. Here it is." Bruce unzipped his backpack and snatched out his pristine copy of *The Victim*. "I wanted to bring this by personally," he explained, pushing the thick sheaf of white paper across the desk, "because I was hoping you'd read it first. I'm not being cocky or anything—I just think it's really good."

Professor Gordon erupted into surprised laughter, and Bruce flinched, terrified that he wasn't being taken seriously.

"I didn't mean that quite the way it came out—"

"Nothing to apologize for, Bruce. A little conviction goes a long way in the movie business." Professor Gordon held the title page up to examine it in the fading light streaming through the office window. "*The Victim*, eh? I'll tell you what," he added with a conspiratorial wink. "I'll get to it as soon as I can."

"I'd appreciate that," Bruce said, relieved. "I'm dying to hear your opinion—as soon as humanly possible."

Professor Gordon nodded and dropped the screenplay on top of the considerable pile on his desk. "Well, don't expect miracles," he warned. "As you can see, I'm kind of busy."

Bruce nodded in awe. "How do you manage to write *and* teach classes too? I barely found time to *breathe* while I was working on *The Victim*."

The professor shrugged. "We all find ways to do what we have to do, Bruce," he said with a smile. "Anyway, drop back by in a couple of days and I'll let you know what I think."

Bruce rose to his feet, excited by Professor Gordon's promise. "I hope you like it," he blurted earnestly as he shouldered his backpack. "If you don't, I'll be totally devastated."

"Not devastated, I hope," Professor Gordon said lightly. "Screenwriting is a tough business, Bruce. If you want to play the game, you have to expect to lose a few rounds. Anyway, this isn't the real deal," he added encouragingly. "It's only a college course."

It's the real deal to me, Bruce thought grimly as the professor's door closed softly behind him. *If Professor Gordon doesn't like that script, I'll never be able to face him again.*

"There!" Jessica said, pushing Elizabeth's copy of *Night Falls Slowly* back into place in her sister's alphabetically arranged bookcase. She could barely wait for Elizabeth to get back from that stupid Journalism Safari or whatever she'd called it and see Professor Gordon's autograph.

Sighing, Jessica looked around the dorm room she shared with her twin and realized that it was still only Monday; Elizabeth wasn't due back from Los Angeles until Sunday. She'd have a long time to wait. And in the meantime how was she supposed to entertain herself?

She could always go over to Theta house, of course, but she was so tired of listening to Lila complain about Bruce all the time. *At least I got out of being on that breakfast committee!* Jessica thought with relief. *Otherwise I'd have to listen to Lila whine first thing every morning.* On the other hand, being on the committee would have given her something to do . . . something other than homework. And homework was all she had to do right now.

"Theta house it is!" she announced to her

reflection as she grabbed a denim jacket off the back of her closet door. She took another second to run a brush through her long blond hair and touch up the mascara around her blue-green eyes before she stepped out into the hall and locked the door to room 28, Dickenson Hall.

After all, she reasoned as she headed toward the staircase, *Lila and Bruce can't fight forever. And Monday-Night Sundae-Nights at Theta house make listening to anyone's complaining easier.*

Bruce turned his key in the lock and opened his apartment door thankfully. Even though it was barely past six, Bruce couldn't remember the last time he'd been so exhausted. Closing the door behind him, he shrugged his backpack off into a chair and headed for the kitchen. The refrigerator was practically empty, but there was a half-full jug of orange juice left. Bruce drank it down greedily and tossed the empty plastic container into the sink.

He left the kitchen and walked into the bedroom, wanting to check his phone messages. *Lila must have gotten all my messages by now,* he thought. *She must have called.* But Bruce couldn't believe his eyes when he got within sight of the answering machine and saw the steady, unblinking light. He didn't have a single message!

"What's her story?" he grumbled under his breath, stretching out on the bed in his darkened bedroom and wondering what to do. If he called her again, he was going to look like a total wimp. On the other hand, he *did* owe her a pretty big apology; she had a right to be mad at him. *But I have a right to be angry too,* Bruce told himself, bitterly remembering the giant bouquet of roses from that loser named Marcus. *If only I hadn't torn up that card with his number on it. I'd call him right now and let him have it.*

Settling his head on one of his pillows, Bruce closed his eyes. *I'll just lie here a few minutes and see if she calls me,* he decided. The walk back to the parking lot and his Porsche from Professor Gordon's office had seemed endless, and even the short drive home had been too long. Staying up two nights in a row had really taken its toll on his mind and body.

It's so annoying of Lila to play these little games, he thought sleepily. *But once Professor Gordon reads my screenplay, he'll totally be blown away—and it'll all be worth it.*

Bruce smiled and wished there was some way for Professor Gordon to instantaneously absorb the script so that they could move directly to the important business of selling it. After putting in all that hard work, why should he have to wait?

Just keep cool, he told himself. *When Professor Gordon—Dennis—helps you get in the business, you'll have plenty of time to hang out with him.* Bruce smiled as he imagined the two of them logging in some power rounds at the golf course, then heading over to the club-house for some martinis. *Maybe I'll even invite Dennis to ride in the limo with me and Lila when Academy Awards time rolls around. . . .*

Bruce felt himself starting to drift, but he didn't fight it. *Lila . . . I'll call you again. But for now . . .* He flipped over on the bedspread, completely comfortable in spite of the fact that he was still fully dressed and wearing cowboy boots.

. . . just a couple of minutes . . .

A moment later he was sound asleep.

Chapter Three

"Lila! Lila, wait up!" The deep male voice rang out clearly across the empty quad, and Lila slowed her steps with a pleased little smile on her face. If she wasn't mistaken, that voice belonged to a very good-looking blond Frisbee player.

"Marcus! What a surprise," she greeted him coolly, admiring how well his full tennis whites emphasized his perfect tan.

"You're up early," he observed, flashing a killer smile when he caught up with her.

"So are you," Lila replied with a glance at her gold watch. It was barely nine in the morning.

"You know what they say—the early bird gets the court." Marcus swung his expensive tennis racket through a shortened forehand. "How about you? What are you up to?"

Lila grimaced. "There are these two *awful*

girls in my sorority," she explained. "We're putting on a charity breakfast for Valley House, and they're ruining *everything*. I have to get to Theta house and make the committee vote on the final plan before they do any more damage."

"What kind of damage?" Marcus asked, an amused glint in his deep brown eyes.

"Who knows?" Lila said irritably. "They could decide we should all wear polyester waitress uniforms. Or serve Spam! You have no idea what I'm up against."

Marcus chuckled. "You might look cute in a polyester waitress uniform." His eyes roamed Lila's body in a way that sent the blood rushing to her cheeks.

"Well, obviously I'd look better in one than Alison or Tina," she returned, embarrassed. "But that's not the point. We're supposed to be raising money for Valley House, not fighting among ourselves."

"You're absolutely right," Marcus agreed, his expression finally serious. "I have to admit, though—I'm a little surprised to find you so passionate about social causes."

Lila tossed her long brown hair. "Why wouldn't I be?"

Marcus hesitated for a second, then shrugged. "Well, to be very blunt, I assumed you were too rich to care."

Lila's eyes widened involuntarily. "But how—"

"Oh, come on, Lila," Marcus said. "Like recognizes like, you know. Don't tell me you haven't noticed that I've got money too?"

Lila shook her head no, an embarrassed little smile on her lips. Normally she was so sure of herself around men, but for some reason Marcus had her completely off-balance. *It's got to be that body,* she decided, sneaking a sidelong look. *Unless, of course, it's those big brown eyes. Maybe both.*

"Anyway, I think it's great that you care so much about helping people," Marcus added.

"You do?" They reached the edge of the quad and stopped walking. Theta house and the tennis courts lay in opposite directions.

"Of course. Most of the girls I know don't worry about anything more important than their clothes."

Lila glanced down self-consciously at her Henri et Garibaldi casual jersey suit and the stack-heeled loafers she'd just bought at Mais Oui.

"I didn't mean you have to wear *ugly* clothes," Marcus clarified, smiling.

"Well . . . thanks," she said uncertainly. "I think." Marcus's smile was so infectious, she found herself returning it.

"So, um . . . how did you like the roses?" Marcus asked brightly. "You haven't said anything about them."

"Excuse me?"

"I sent you red roses yesterday," Marcus explained urgently, looking thoroughly crushed. "Don't tell me they didn't deliver them!"

"Those were from you?"

Marcus heaved a sigh of apparent relief. "Of course. Didn't you read the card?"

"There *was* no card," Lila said slowly. She still hadn't had a chance to look at that enormous pink epic of Bruce's, but she'd added water to the flowers. She was sure there had been no card anywhere.

"What a drag," Marcus said. "I went to the florist to write it myself. They must have forgotten to put it in."

"Yes, probably," Lila agreed. But she had her own suspicions about what had happened to that card. Bruce had been at her doorstep with that stupid screenplay—he must have stolen the card so that she'd think the flowers were from *him!* It had almost worked too. *What a snake,* Lila steamed, hungry for payback.

She turned her most charming, flirtatious smile on Marcus. "I owe you a thank-you, then," she said. "The flowers are beautiful."

Marcus seemed satisfied with her reaction. "I'm glad you like them. They seemed right for you somehow."

"I've always *loved* roses."

"Really? How do you feel about filet mignon?" Marcus asked. "I know a great steak house at the beach."

"Are you asking me out?" Lila said, taken aback. It was one thing to flirt with him a little, but something else entirely to actually *date* him.

"Tomorrow night at six?" he answered.

He certainly moves fast, she thought, even while the hopeful expression on his face was melting her resistance. "I don't know if that's such a good idea," Lila stalled. "We barely know each other." *Not to mention the fact that I'm seeing someone already*, she added to herself. *Neglectful or not, Bruce is still my boyfriend. On the other hand, he does need to be taught a lesson. . . .*

"Then how about a movie instead?" Marcus persisted. "We'll work our way up to dinner."

Lila paused. "OK."

"Great!" Marcus exclaimed. "I'll call you tonight to set it all up."

Lila watched Marcus's back as he walked away down the path toward the tennis courts and felt a pang of guilt over not telling him about Bruce. But at the thought of her so-called boyfriend, Lila's eyes narrowed dangerously. She hadn't had a chance to return Bruce's calls, and now she had no intention of doing so—not after discovering the truth about the roses.

"Let him sweat," she muttered.

"Don't forget!" Professor Walden chirped as she dismissed Bruce's Tuesday afternoon biology class. "Our second midterm is next week!"

Bruce groaned internally as he stuffed the heavy biology text into his backpack. He'd spent so much time writing *The Victim* that he was way behind in all his other classes. Short of a miracle, he'd probably flunk the test.

But then again, I'm no stranger to bad grades, Bruce thought as he shouldered his heavy pack and stood watching his fellow students file out of the enormous, auditorium-style lecture hall. *Only a professor like Dennis Gordon can get me psyched about doing well in class. And Professor Walden, you're no Dennis Gordon.*

Bruce was aching to go home and kick back, but deep down he knew that if he didn't at least get a little catching up done in each of his classes, he was going to be in serious trouble. Still, the thought of dragging himself over to the library practically put him asleep on his feet. *It wouldn't be so bad if I had Lila to study with me,* he thought, but Lila still hadn't returned any of his calls. And if she wanted to play hardball, he could hold out as long as she could . . . or so he hoped.

With a sigh Bruce started walking in the direction of the nearest exit. *It's study or die, Patman,* he told himself as he emerged into the bright sunshine. The campus was bathed in the warm afternoon light, and students everywhere were relaxing on the lawns as Bruce trudged toward the library. It didn't seem fair that everyone else was through with their classes and having a good time while he still had hours and hours of work to do.

This must be how Elizabeth Wakefield feels every day, he thought as he opened one of the heavy library doors and stepped into the gloom. *No,* he corrected himself, *Elizabeth likes to study.* Bruce shook his head in amazement at the notion.

He stood in the lobby, uncertain where he wanted to sit. There was a pretty good place on the second floor, but all his fraternity brothers hung out there. He wouldn't get anything done if he ran into one of them. The basement was full of those individual study carrels, but the attached seats were uncomfortable, and besides, Bruce couldn't think of anything more depressing than sitting in the basement. *When I sell my script, no one will care if I failed biology,* he told himself, seriously considering blowing the midterm off. But then he had a better idea.

The film department had its own small library—he could study there! Without a second thought Bruce pushed back out through the front doors of the main library and headed for the film and telecommunications buildings. A few minutes later he'd arrived and taken a table by himself next to a huge picture window. It was almost as good as being outside. Bruce opened his backpack wide and began placing everything on the table in front of him.

The pink-and-white copy of *The Victim* beckoned to Bruce, making him realize he would far rather reread his own work than do any of the things he was *supposed* to do. *When is Professor Gordon going to let me know what he thinks?* he wondered anxiously. *It hasn't even been twenty-four hours, and already the suspense is killing me.*

Sighing, Bruce lifted the movie script and placed it on the extreme left edge of the table, next to a couple of stacks of unshelved library books. *Out of sight, out of mind,* he hoped. Then he lined up his notepads in a row in front of him and pushed them out to the far edge of the table. Finally he placed the statistics book to his right and opened the biology book in front of him.

"In any controlled population of normal and curly-winged fruit flies rigorous, repeatable studies indicate that mutations will occur at a rate that corresponds to the ratio among the population of the curly-winged type. . . ."

Bruce's eyes glazed over. No wonder he was having trouble in biology! With every living thing in the entire world to choose from, the geniuses behind the curriculum had decided to study fruit flies. *Who cares?* he wanted to scream.

He looked up from his textbook and inadvertently caught the eye of a tall blond guy working on something at the next table. Bruce recognized him from screenwriting class and looked quickly away, embarrassed that he couldn't think of his name. He must have heard Professor Gordon call on the guy at some point, but he was drawing a total blank.

Bruce dropped his gaze back to his biology text. He hadn't even found his place when a movement on the other side of the picture window caught his attention. Professor Gordon was hurrying past the window, about to turn in the door and most likely head for his office. Jumping to his feet, Bruce grabbed his texts and notepads, stuffing them hurriedly into his backpack. If he ran, he could catch Professor Gordon and see if he'd read *The Victim* yet.

Full backpack in hand, Bruce sprinted across the film library, earning dirty looks from a couple of graduate students as he exploded out the front doors. "Professor Gordon," Bruce shouted, running through the lobby after his teacher. "Professor Gordon!"

The professor stopped walking and waited for Bruce to catch up. "Hello, Mr. Patman," he said with a wry smile. "Something on your mind?"

Bruce struggled to regain his breath. "No. Well . . . yes. Have you . . . have you read my script?" he gasped.

Professor Gordon shook his head with a sympathetic smile. "I know it's torture when you're waiting for those reviews to come in, but I warned you I was busy. I'm afraid I haven't even looked at it yet."

Bruce tried to hide his disappointment, but to no avail. "Do you think you might get to it tomorrow?" he begged pathetically before he could stop himself. "I understand how busy you are, but I'm dying to know what you think. It really doesn't take that long to read, not once you get started."

Professor Gordon shifted his briefcase to his other hand and glanced restlessly in the direction of the elevators. "I'll try, Bruce. I really will. But right now I'm late for a department meeting. If I don't get there in another minute, the rest of the faculty will have me for dinner. All right?"

"Sure," Bruce said weakly as Professor Gordon hurried off, the elevator doors shutting behind him with a resounding *whoosh-thump*.

"A couple more days of this," Bruce muttered to himself, "and I'll go stark raving mad."

"The motion carries," Lila announced triumphantly the next morning, exchanging a satisfied look with Isabella. "That takes care of the date, the venue, the menu, the ticket price, and the publicity campaign. This meeting of the Charity Breakfast Committee is hereby adjourned." She watched with happy relief as all the Thetas on the committee, with the exception of Isabella Ricci, got up and left the room.

"Well, it looks like we did it," Lila told

Isabella, secure at last in her outmaneuvering of Tina and Alison Quinn.

"*You* did it," Isabella corrected. "That was truly awe-inspiring."

Lila laughed, savoring her victory. "It does feel good," she admitted. She came out from behind the podium and began collecting her things in preparation for her Wednesday morning classes. "It took almost two entire days of my life, but it was worth it."

Isabella swept up her black leather backpack, and the two friends walked out of Theta house together into a late morning fog. "Have you talked to Bruce yet?" Isabella asked.

Lila flinched but recovered quickly. "No, and I don't know if I want to. As a matter of fact," she added smoothly, "I have a date with Marcus Stanton tonight."

Isabella stopped dead in the middle of the sidewalk. "You do not!"

"He's taking me to the movies," Lila confirmed without breaking stride.

Isabella had to run a few steps to catch up. "I don't believe it," she protested. "What about Bruce?"

Lila shrugged. "What about him?"

Bruce hurried across the darkening campus Wednesday evening, his heart pounding with excitement. Until now the day had been a total waste.

Lila still hadn't called, he'd read biology until visions of fruit flies danced in his head, and he'd even gotten semi–caught up on his statistics problems. But that was *before* he'd heard the message from Professor Gordon on his answering machine.

"I've read your script," Professor Gordon's tape-recorded voice had said simply. *"If you want to drop by my office around six-thirty tonight, we can discuss it."*

Did he want to drop by?

Was water wet?

Bruce was flushed and panting by the time he reached the hallway outside Professor Gordon's office. He stopped several doors away and took a few deep breaths to calm himself. It had only been two days since he'd turned in his screenplay, but it felt more like a couple of years. And now he was finally going to hear his mentor's opinion. His entire career was in Professor Gordon's hands.

Bruce squared his shoulders and walked the remaining steps to Professor Gordon's door, knocking sharply.

"Come in," called the professor. "Ah, Bruce," he added as Bruce poked his head inside. "I see you got my message. Please, have a seat."

Professor Gordon gestured toward the same leather chair Bruce had occupied two days previously, and Bruce crossed to it eagerly, sitting forward on its edge.

"So, Bruce," Professor Gordon said. "Where to begin? I've never read anything quite like *The Victim*."

"Really?" Bruce said excitedly.

"No, it's refreshingly unique. I give you high marks for originality."

"That's what *I* thought!" Bruce straightened up, hanging on the professor's every word.

"You obviously put a lot of work into it—"

"Tons! I missed so many dates with my girlfriend that she's not even speaking to me anymore."

"Well, your devotion to your art is commendable," the professor said, an amused smile on his face.

Bruce beamed. "And?"

"And some of your characterizations are interesting," Professor Gordon continued. "I was especially intrigued by your main character, the murder victim—"

"Miles Lockwood," Bruce butted in, unable to keep from interrupting again.

Professor Gordon smiled. "Right. One does feel a certain sympathy for the poor devil."

Professor Gordon liked Miles Lockwood! Bruce thought triumphantly. "I wanted to make him a tragic figure," Bruce explained, unable to shake the cheer from his voice. "You know, a guy who does his best but still can't win."

The professor picked up a pencil from his desk and wiggled it thoughtfully between his thumb and middle finger. "Yes. I think Miles comes off as extremely tragic."

Bruce snorted. "Sure, because he *dies!*" He relaxed back into his chair a little, enjoying the moment. Not only had he totally aced the assignment, but he was obviously on his way to Hollywood. Still, there was no major hurry—not just now anyway. Bruce could afford to let his buddy Dennis ramble on for a while about how great *The Victim* was before he asked the professor to call his agent.

"Exactly. He dies. And I suppose death is always tragic, even though the events that led to Miles's eventual demise didn't seem particularly likely."

If his agent reads it tomorrow, I wonder if he can sell it the same day? Bruce wondered. *Well, no. It'll probably take a little longer for the studio heads to look it over and make their offers. . . . Hey! Wait a minute!*

"Did you say 'not particularly likely'?" Bruce asked, not sure he'd heard correctly.

The professor smiled apologetically. "Of course in a movie, anything can happen. But the audience must *believe* Miles's death can happen and must *want* it to happen."

"So you don't think the audience will want Miles to die?" Bruce asked, wondering how he could rewrite the ending.

A smile flickered around the corners of Professor

Gordon's mouth. "Well . . . not exactly. You see, I'm quite sure the audience *will* want Miles to die. Perhaps not for the reasons you've intended."

A small gasp escaped Bruce's lips as the truth hit him with the force of a blow to the solar plexus. His script wasn't any good! Professor Gordon was just looking for a way to let him down easy. The room seemed suddenly too small, too hot, too lacking in oxygen. "You *really* didn't like it, did you?" Bruce managed, his voice half choked with shock and disappointment.

"I'm sorry," Professor Gordon said gently. "I know you were excited about it, so I tried to find something to recommend it. But the whole plot is just too far-fetched. The twists are jarring and, I'm afraid, absurd. Where is the motivation? Where is the conflict?"

"The guy's been poisoned," Bruce argued desperately. "If he doesn't find his killer and the antidote in time, he'll die. Isn't that enough conflict?"

"Where are the police?" Professor Gordon continued calmly. "You can't really expect an audience to believe that poor Miles has no recourse but to find his own killer?"

"He's dying. There's no time—"

"Bruce. I understand how hard it is to let go of a project after you've put so much of yourself into it, but my candid advice is to scrap this one. It's just too flawed to save."

Bruce slumped in his chair, his mind reeling, his hopes shattered. Embarrassment crushed him like a lead elephant.

"Perhaps screenwriting isn't your forte," Professor Gordon suggested kindly. "It's not for everyone, you know."

"Apparently not." Bruce forced himself to smile as if he didn't care, but inside he was heartbroken. "At least I didn't make copies for all my friends," he added, imagining how humiliating it would have been to have to go around and ask for them all back. *"Excuse me,"* he heard himself saying, *"could I have my screenplay back? I thought it was the next* Night Falls Slowly, *but I just found out I'm a no-talent hack."* No, at least he'd been spared that disgrace. He hadn't shown *The Victim* to anyone except Professor Gordon.

And Lila, he remembered suddenly, wincing.

"Is something the matter?" Professor Gordon asked.

"I just remembered—I *did* give out one other copy, to my girlfriend. I hope she hasn't read it yet. She'd probably hate it even more than you did."

"Well, it's not the end of the world," Professor Gordon said.

"It is if I failed," Bruce moaned. "What's my grade?"

Professor Gordon leaned back in his chair

and folded his hands over his sweater vest. "I never reveal grades before I hand back the work in class. But if it makes you feel any better, I'll tell you in advance that you're getting a passing grade for trying so hard."

"Thanks." It *didn't* make him feel any better, but he supposed it was better than nothing.

"Rejection is part of being a writer, you know. You learn to take these things in stride."

"Sure," Bruce agreed, his eyes on the carpet. Like he was ever going to write anything ever again!

"You're taking this too hard," the professor insisted. "I'll tell you what. Why don't you join me for a Scotch? I confess I used to treat myself to an entire bottle after every major rejection. For a tiny setback like this, though, a large glass should suffice."

Bruce looked up, surprised. *Is this really only a tiny setback?* he wondered. Then he realized that Professor Gordon was still just trying to cheer him up. A glass of Scotch was probably his idea of some sort of consolation prize. Still, it was nice to know that the professor hadn't pegged him for a *total* loser.

"Sure," Bruce said, nodding his acceptance. He didn't really like Scotch, but in Professor Gordon's sophisticated, culture-laden office, it seemed like the intellectually masculine thing to do.

Professor Gordon reached behind him, lifted a couple of cut-crystal glasses off the credenza, and filled them halfway. Bruce took one of the glasses, feeling its weight in his hand. He stared unhappily into its warm amber depths for a moment, then tossed down a couple of quick, fiery swallows.

The professor regarded Bruce with concern. "You're not too upset, are you?" he asked solicitously, putting down his glass.

"I'm fine," Bruce lied, surprised to feel the beginnings of tears burning unexpectedly behind his eyes—tears that were only half Scotch induced. The thought of crying in front of Professor Gordon made Bruce so nervous that he hurriedly gulped down as much of his Scotch as he could, barely tasting it. A sweat broke out on his upper lip as the potent liquor raged down his throat.

"Excellent," he gasped. He put the glass down on the adjacent windowsill, pushing it back behind the drapery so Professor Gordon wouldn't notice he hadn't quite emptied it.

"I'm glad you liked it," the professor replied.

"Mmm, yes. It was, uh, very smooth. I'd better get going now, though. I want to get that screenplay back from Lila before she reads it." Bruce stood and took one last, longing look around Professor Gordon's opulent office, knowing he'd probably never see it again.

"Stop by anytime," Professor Gordon offered, as if reading his thoughts.

"Yeah. Thanks." Like he actually would! Bruce rushed out the door and into the hallway as the sweat began to trickle down his forehead.

It was cooler in the hallway—cooler still outside the film building. But the fresh night air didn't clear Bruce's head as he rushed across campus to the parking lot. *Way to go, Patman,* he taunted himself. *You've just made a total fool of yourself in front of the most important professor on campus.*

"So much for becoming the next Quentin Tarantino," Bruce grumbled as he leaped in his Porsche. "Now if I want to work in the film industry, it'll have to be behind the counter of a video store—if I'm *lucky,* that is."

Bruce gunned his powerful engine and gripped the steering wheel tightly. There were times when driving his car at top speed made him forget all his problems, but Bruce knew instinctively that tonight wasn't going to be one of them. It was going to take a lot more than a fast car to make him feel better. It was going to take . . .

"Lila," he groaned, pulling out of the parking lot. What a fool he'd been! All this game playing . . . who called who last . . . suddenly it all made him feel sick. He didn't care about the last two weeks anymore. He didn't even care that some jerk named Marcus had sent her flowers. All he wanted to do was hold her, bury his face in her fragrant hair, and forget everything bad that had ever happened to him.

"Oh, Lila," he repeated, turning the Porsche in the direction of her apartment. "I really need you right now. Please be there for me."

Chapter Four

"Oh, Bruce," Lila muttered under her breath. She ran the mascara wand through her thick lashes one last time, surveying the results in her bathroom mirror. "I wish you could see what you're missing."

Perfect, she thought. *As usual.* Her chestnut hair was pinned up with only a few strategically placed strands cascading down, her makeup was flawless, and the dress she had on was brand-new, just arrived from that cute little boutique in Paris. Lila looked good—she knew it—but she was surprised to discover that for once, it didn't make her all that happy.

"Stupid Bruce," she grumbled, annoyed. "Stupid, childish, selfish, conceited, pain-in-the-butt Bruce!"

Why did he have to make everything so hard? On Tuesday, when Lila had accepted this date with Marcus, she'd still been so angry with Bruce that it had seemed like a good idea. But now, only one day later, she was having second thoughts.

She walked into her bedroom and bent to smell Marcus's roses, which she had moved onto her dresser. The red roses were in spectacular full bloom now, and she breathed their fragrance in deeply, hoping it would calm her doubts. *Marcus is a nice guy, and nothing's going to happen that I don't want to happen,* Lila reassured herself. *Anyway, it's too late to back out now.*

Leaving her bedroom, she walked into the living room and began pacing restlessly. She hated this part of a date—the part where she was completely ready and she didn't even want to sit down for fear of wrinkling her dress. As she paced she noticed Bruce's untouched manuscript still sitting on her coffee table. *I don't even know why he gave me that stupid thing,* she thought irritably. As far as Lila was concerned, the screenplay was the cause of all the problems between them. *Did Bruce actually expect me to sift through that monstrosity?*

Still, it would *be interesting to see what Bruce wasted two whole weeks of his life on,* Lila mused as she circuited around her living room a few more times, every few seconds letting her eyes dart over toward the sheaf of pink paper.

Finally curiosity overcame her and she furtively picked up the thick manuscript.

"*The Victim*, by Bruce Patman," she read aloud. "Gee, Bruce, could you have put your name in bigger print?" Rolling her eyes, she flipped to the second page.

"Dedicated to Lila Fowler, the love of my life and the most beautiful woman I've ever known."

Tears sprang to Lila's eyes. It was corny—no doubt about that—but Lila couldn't deny that Bruce's dedication touched her just the same. Sure, Bruce could be a pigheaded jerk sometimes, but he was the pigheaded jerk she loved.

She sighed, picturing him alone at his apartment, sitting by the phone and waiting for her to call him. But instead of finding joy in that pathetic image, Lila now wished that she could transport herself to his front door that very instant, slip inside, and surprise him with a long, spine-tingling kiss. A dreamy smile came over Lila's face as she closed her eyes and let herself become absorbed in the fantasy.

"Hello?" called a voice through her open window. "Lila?"

"Marcus!" Lila exclaimed, startled back into reality. She dropped Bruce's script guiltily back onto the coffee table. "Come on in."

Marcus stepped inside, his brilliant white smile nearly blinding her. He was wearing khakis and a lavender polo shirt, and Lila barely had time to realize it was the first time she'd seen him in long pants before he extended a huge bouquet of mixed spring flowers in her direction. "You look beautiful," he said.

"Thank you," she responded, unexpectedly flustered by the compliment. She took the flowers from Marcus's hands and stood staring at them blankly, completely disoriented by the strangeness of having someone other than Bruce picking her up for a date.

"I know what you're thinking," Marcus offered with a laugh. "Flowers twice in one week isn't very original. But you're in such good shape, I was pretty sure you didn't eat chocolate."

Lila smiled. Marcus was wrong about the chocolate, but he certainly knew how to get on a girl's good side. "The flowers are beautiful. I'm just going to put them in some water."

Marcus followed her into the kitchen, chatting happily. "I hope you like the movie," he said. "The reviews have been kind of mixed."

"I'm sure it'll be great." Lila opened a cupboard and stretched up on her toes to lift down a vase from the uppermost shelf. It was a little too high, and she couldn't quite get her fingers around it.

"Let me do that!" Marcus intervened. He came to her side and retrieved the vase easily. When he turned to hand it to her, however, Lila found herself suddenly standing so close to him that she could smell his aftershave. There wasn't even enough room between them for the vase.

"Oh. Sorry," he apologized, taking a step backward and holding out the vase. "Close quarters."

"Yes," Lila agreed, feeling the heat rise up in her face. "It's a small kitchen."

She busied herself with the flowers at the sink, grateful for the excuse to turn her back on Marcus for a minute. What was she supposed to do? How was she supposed to feel? Everything about Marcus spoke of class and wealth—his clothes, his manners, that perfect, movie-star smile. He was the first guy Lila had encountered at SVU who could even hold a candle to Bruce, but this guy's candle was more like a searchlight. It was almost too broad and bright. It overwhelmed her in a way that she wasn't sure was good or bad.

Lila's hands shook as she trimmed the flower stems one at a time, trying to regain her composure. For a second there, when they'd been standing face-to-face only inches apart, she'd had this wild, almost overwhelming desire to *kiss* him.

Just like you wanted to kiss Bruce a few moments ago, she scolded herself as she put Marcus's last flower into the vase. *This isn't right. You should call this whole date off right now . . . and then you should call your boyfriend.*

"There," she said weakly, pushing aside her internal confusion and holding out the bouquet

63

for Marcus to admire. "What do you think?"

"Gorgeous," he replied. "Just like you." He smiled and held out one tanned hand. "Are you ready to go?"

No! Lila's conscience screamed. She smiled at him weakly, half mesmerized by his eyes in spite of her doubts. *It's just a movie,* she reassured herself. *Nothing bad ever happens in the movies, right?*

"OK. Let's go," she said, swallowing her doubts as she put her hand in his.

Bruce pulled his car up the alley behind Lila's apartment complex and parked right next to a big metal Dumpster. Normally he wouldn't have left his precious Porsche anywhere near there, but it was the closest he could get to Lila's place, and he was desperate to see her.

He had never felt so desolate before, so completely alone in the world. Professor Gordon's rejection hurt more than Bruce would have believed possible, and he was starting to understand why. He'd been so certain that his script would be a hit, that the rest of his life would be filled with excitement, celebrities, and adoring fans. Now, in less than an hour, the dream was gone. Dead. Murdered in its infancy.

Slamming the car door behind him, Bruce dashed through the alleyway to the front of Lila's building and vaulted up her dark front porch.

The only light in the courtyard came from the six little sidewalk lanterns that lit the main pathway, one at each junction of the short, individual walkways to the six separate cottages. Squinting, Bruce knocked on Lila's door, gently calling, "Lila, are you there?"

When she didn't answer, he pounded against the door with the side of his fist and rang the bell at the same time. "Lila! Open up!" Still no answer.

She wasn't home. He knew it, but he didn't want to believe it. "Lila!" He was using both fists now, pounding as if he would break the door down. "Lila, let me in!"

"Lila's not home," said a female voice from the path behind him. "So how about knocking that off?"

Stopping immediately, Bruce turned to face what appeared to be a young woman, though it was hard to see in the dim light of the lanterns. Bruce could only vaguely make out a lumpy chenille bathrobe and wide, frightened eyes. *She's afraid of you,* he thought in disbelief before the still-sane half of his brain kicked in. *No wonder. You're acting like a total psycho.*

"I'm sorry I bothered you," Bruce said, trying to make his voice calm and reasonable. The door of the unit across from Lila's was open, emitting a sliver of light, and Bruce guessed the woman in the bathrobe must have come from there. "Do you know where Lila is?" he asked.

"No," the girl answered quickly. "And if I did, I wouldn't tell you."

Why wasn't he surprised? "Look, I'll level with you," he said. "Lila and I have been fighting, but it's over now. I'm only here to apologize."

"All I can say is, it must have been some fight," she observed, turning and walking back toward her apartment.

"Why do you say that?" Bruce called after her.

"Because the guy she left with was a *total* babe." The woman shut the door behind her, ending the conversation.

Bruce winced as her words seemed to slap him in the face. Lila was out with someone else! How could she do that to him? Who would she even go out with? Then, in a flash of intuition, Bruce knew.

Marcus.

He could imagine what had happened. While Bruce had been holed up in his apartment day and night, Marcus had been keeping Lila company. Maybe their romance had started with a cup of coffee after class or an offer to dance at one of those stupid Theta parties Bruce had missed. *It doesn't matter how it started*, Bruce realized, despair knotting his stomach. *I should have known how it would end.*

He stood staring at Lila's door for a few more minutes, wondering if he would ever be welcomed through it again. The idea made his stomach burn and his heart turn to ice. Crushed, his head hanging low in defeat, Bruce wandered back through the desolate alleyway to his car. His screenplay was a joke, his girlfriend was cheating on him, and—to make things even worse—he was starting to suspect that it was all his fault.

If only I'd called Lila back on Sunday night like I promised! he chastised himself as he squeezed past the Dumpster to get to his Porsche. *But* no, *I had to be so completely wrapped up in writing that—that piece of trash.*

In a fit of sudden anger Bruce flung open his car door and grabbed his backpack out of the passenger seat. The perfect resting place for his own copy of *The Victim* was right nearby—the Dumpster. *No better place for garbage,* he told himself, tearing at the zippers of his backpack savagely and finally spilling everything out onto the driver's seat. Books, papers, and pens overflowed onto the floorboards. But the screenplay wasn't there.

Bruce stared at the mess openmouthed, dumbfounded. What happened to his stupid script? His stomach churned at the thought of some total stranger coming across it and rolling on the floor with laughter as they read it. With a groan of resignation Bruce shoved everything violently over to the passenger side of the Porsche and sank into the driver's seat.

"Things don't just fall out of zippered backpacks," he told himself, hoping he was right. He must have taken the screenplay out and forgotten it somewhere. But where? Bruce stretched his memory, trying to think of the last time he'd seen his own pink-and-white copy of *The Victim*.

"At the film library!" he remembered after a moment. Of course. He must have accidentally left it behind when he'd sprinted out of the room to catch Professor Gordon. Disgusted, Bruce slammed the car door shut and turned the key in the ignition, wondering if the film library would keep bad screenplays in the lost and found or just toss them in the wastebasket where they belonged.

But knowing that a copy of his bad screenplay—with his *name* on it!—was floating around out there somewhere was *nothing* compared to the fear of losing his girlfriend. Bruce squeezed his burning eyes shut against the pain of envisioning Lila in someone else's arms. The mere idea of it made him insane with jealousy.

"You'll get her back," he said, his breathing fast and shallow. He opened his eyes and pulled the Porsche out into the alley, barely aware of the pavement rolling by under his wheels. Of course he'd get her back. He *had* to.

But what if Lila didn't want him anymore?

"That's crazy," he told himself angrily. "Everything's going to be like it was before." He thought for a moment as he took a sharp turn onto the main road back to his apartment building. "But if I ever run into that guy Marcus," he added matter-of-factly, "I'm going to have to kill him."

"Where do you usually like to sit?" Marcus asked as he and Lila pushed through the swinging door into the nearly empty theater. "In the back? The front? Somewhere in the middle?"

Lila surveyed the rows of empty seats from where she stood at the top of the aisle. "It looks like we have our pick," she said noncommittally. *Bruce would have known where I wanted to sit*, she couldn't help thinking. Of course Bruce would also have known that she really wanted to see the movie showing next door, that she always drank diet soda and liked her popcorn dripping with extra butter, and that she never, *never* ate those awful juju things.

"Let's sit in the back," Marcus suggested, beginning to edge his way down the very last row. With a shrug Lila followed.

"I always like it back here the best," he added as they reached the center of the back row and dropped into two adjacent red velvet seats. "It's more private."

"Um . . . it certainly is," Lila agreed, glancing

around anxiously. Actually, the back row looked a little *too* private. The rear wall of the theater was directly behind them, and there was no one sitting in front of them for several rows. Lila nibbled on some popcorn to cover her nervousness.

"I wouldn't have pegged you for an extra-butter kind of girl," Marcus teased. "But I'm glad you are."

Their hands brushed as Marcus reached into the tub, and Lila recoiled slightly involuntarily. *This is a huge mistake,* she thought miserably as Marcus casually chomped on his popcorn as if going out with her was something he did every day. When the house lights went down, her stomach clenched as she realized that she was in for the long haul. No matter how hard she tried, she couldn't suppress the feeling that something here just wasn't right.

Bruce Patman—that's what isn't right, Lila realized. *Bruce messed up, but at least he wasn't with another girl. What I'm doing to him is worse than what he did to me.*

Lila snuck a glimpse at Marcus out of the corner of her eye—his handsome face was illuminated in bursts by a series of explosive car crashes featured in the coming attractions. He was still just as good-looking, just as refined, but suddenly he wasn't as attractive anymore. In fact, Lila was starting to wonder what she'd ever even seen in him.

Way worse, she amended, shrinking down in her seat.

Jessica lunged across her dorm room toward the telephone, grabbing it in the middle of the very first ring. "Hellooo?" she shouted extravagantly into the receiver.

"Jeez, Jess. Expecting a call from the president?"

"Oh, it's you, Steven." Even though Jessica was happy to hear from her big brother, she was disappointed that it wasn't one of her girlfriends calling to see if she wanted to go out somewhere and have some fun.

"Try to contain your excitement," Steven replied.

"I *am* excited," Jessica protested unconvincingly. "It's just that it's so *boring* here with Elizabeth gone. Isabella's out with Danny, Lila isn't answering her phone, and I can't hang out at Theta house *every* night—it would look too pathetic."

"I'd be enjoying the peace and privacy if I were you," Steven said.

"Yeah, right! As if peace and privacy were really my speed, Steven. Besides, this place is a total dump." Jessica looked with disgust around her messy, confining dorm room as if she could somehow send Steven a mental picture through the telephone.

71

"Well, I'm sure *half* of it's a dump anyway," Steven teased. "The other half probably looks pretty good."

"Very funny." Why did everyone always make such a big deal out of the fact that Elizabeth was a just teensy bit neater than she was? "Is that why you called? To insult me?"

"No, actually I just called to see if you wanted to hang out with me and a couple of my friends tonight at the Blue Lagoon," Steven replied, naming a dive bar near campus that was popular with the grad-school crowd. "But since you're obviously having such a great time at home, I guess I shouldn't bother you."

"Um, would that be a couple of your *law-school* friends?" Jessica asked, perking up immediately. The law-school crowd was older and more sophisticated—not to mention that a few of those guys were *extremely* hot.

"Do I have any other kind?" Steven quipped. "No, really, Jess. How about it? We're just going to stop by there later for an hour or so."

"Hmmm. I'll have to think about it," she replied, trying to force a bored tone into her voice. The last thing she needed was to let Steven know how thrilled she was about his invitation.

"C'mon. They have great chicken wings," he coaxed.

"Well, I *guess* I could fit that in," Jessica

drawled, her heart pounding excitedly. She began darting around the room in an attempt to seek out just the right outfit as she impatiently listened to Steven relay the final details of time and place.

"Yes, yes. I've got it," Jessica interrupted after a minute. "I'll see you there."

Jessica hung up the phone hastily and danced over to her closet, pulling out her bathrobe and shower kit, a satisfied smile on her face. She had a whole lot of bathing, primping, and natural beautifying to do before she met up with all those sexy future lawyers.

"Well, what did you think?" Marcus asked when the house lights came up. "*I* thought it was abominable. One of the ten worst movies I've seen all year."

Lila found herself smiling—the movie *was* pretty bad. "I'm afraid I'll have to agree with you."

"Well, not everyone can write a decent screenplay, that's for sure."

Lila's good mood disappeared as quickly as it came. *Why, of all things, would Marcus have to mention screenplays?* she griped silently. *I feel guilty enough about Bruce already.*

"So what should we do now?" he asked as they walked out to the lobby. "It's still early."

"I don't know . . . ," Lila hedged.

"How about getting some coffee? I know this great little place not far from here."

Lila remained silent, her head swimming with excuses, until they had stepped outside into the cool night air. "I—I don't think so, Marcus. I should really be getting home. I've got a major class load on Thursday mornings," she lied.

"We don't have to stay long."

"Maybe another time."

"Just one cup!" Marcus begged, a hint of desperation creeping into his handsome brown eyes.

The desperation clinched it for Lila. She didn't *want* to have coffee with him—not now, not ever. And what Marcus needed, more than anything, was to know that. *Now.*

"I'm sorry, Marcus, but I want to go home," Lila insisted. "You seem like a nice guy, but the truth is, I never should have let things go this far. I already have a boyfriend."

"A boyfriend?" Marcus repeated, looking stunned. "Why didn't you say so before?"

Lila shrugged apologetically. How could she tell him when she was wondering the exact same thing? "I *should* have," she managed. "It's just that he and I are fighting. And you seemed so nice and everything . . . I figured it wouldn't hurt to give you a chance. But—but I'm afraid this was all a bad idea. I'm sorry."

"I don't believe it," Marcus protested. "We were having such a great time together!"

Lila's eyes widened. Had the two of them been on the same date? "It's just not going to work out. I still love my boyfriend."

Marcus shook his head, as if trying to wake himself from a particularly bad dream. "So you're dumping me? Is that it?"

"No! How could I dump you, Marcus? We're not even dating!"

Marcus's cheeks flushed deeply and his brown eyes flashed angrily. "I thought you were nice," he said, his voice low and clipped. "I guess I was wrong."

Lila could feel her own cheeks reddening with embarrassment as passersby on the sidewalk slowed their steps to listen and stare. "Well . . . I'm sorry," she repeated nervously. "You know what? You don't have to drive me home. I'll just call a cab."

"Stop—I'll drive you," Marcus shouted as Lila hurried back toward the theater lobby, leaving him standing by himself on the sidewalk. "Don't be ridiculous!"

"No, that's OK," she blurted over her shoulder before she pushed through the lobby doors. "I don't want to be any trouble."

"Too late for *that*," Marcus shot back bitterly.

The heavy glass door closed behind her, blocking out any further protests from Marcus. Lila hurried over to the pay phones, all the while keeping a covert eye on Marcus through the windows. He stood steaming on the sidewalk, his hands clenched into fists.

"Please be there," Lila prayed, dropping a quarter into the slot and dialing Bruce's number. Her temples throbbed in time with the quick pace of her heart as she tried to ignore Marcus's angry gaze through the window. The way he was staring at her was actually starting to scare her now. "Come on, Bruce. Answer the phone," she muttered.

The line picked up. *"This is Bruce—you know the drill,"* his answering machine barked, startling her. With a shaking hand Lila pressed down the hook and fumbled through her purse for another quarter. She could feel the heat of Marcus's eyes on her back, flustering her. When she finally snagged a second quarter, she dropped it in the slot and dialed Dickenson Hall. Maybe Jessica would be home. *Hopefully* she'd be home.

"Come *on*, Jess." She took in an excited breath when the phone picked up, but before she could speak, she was cut off by, *"Hi! This is Elizabeth."* *"And Jessica!"* *"Please leave us a—"* Groaning, Lila slammed down the receiver and began considering her scant options.

Lila certainly didn't mind spending money on a cab; it was just that she didn't want to go anywhere—especially home—*alone*. Not with Marcus looking as if he was mentally throwing daggers into her back every time she peered over her shoulder. But she had no other choice. Reluctantly Lila found another quarter and dialed a third number.

"B&B Taxi!" chirped a pleasant voice.

"I need a cab to pick me up at the Cineplex," Lila said. "Tell the driver I'm waiting in the lobby and to pull up as close as he can."

"No problem!" responded the voice. "We'll have someone there in five minutes."

"Thanks." Lila replaced the telephone receiver and took a deep breath. *Everything is under control,* she told herself. *Marcus just got his feelings a little hurt, that's all. He'll get over it.* In the meantime she was in a crowded public place and her taxi was on its way. She was perfectly safe; it was silly to be afraid. Squaring her shoulders, Lila stepped away from the telephone and turned to face the sidewalk.

Marcus was gone.

Chapter Five

That place looks depressing enough, Bruce thought as he eyed the seedy old bar from the sidewalk. The sign over the Blue Lagoon was on the blink—literally. The ugly blue neon letters flickered on and off erratically as Bruce pushed through the grimy double doors and into the dark interior.

The bar seemed pretty crowded for a Wednesday night, and Bruce recognized more than a few people from around SVU. Pushing his way up to the bar, he was amazed to see an empty stool. He dropped onto it gratefully.

"Give me a draft," Bruce barked at the bartender. "Anything to take my mind off Lila," he murmured under the blaring noise of the jukebox. Bruce had gone home after he'd left Lila's apartment, but the silence there had been so overwhelming that he'd left the Porsche behind, choosing to walk to the nearest dive and get plastered.

The bartender did his part by pushing a sloppy, wet mug across the bar in Bruce's direction. "How about you?" he asked the guy on the stool next to Bruce's. "You ready for another?"

"Yeah. Fill 'em up!" the guy slurred, using the back of his right arm to slide several empty mugs back toward the bartender. "Fill 'em all up."

The bartender removed the empty mugs, dropping them into a sink full of suds beneath the bar. He fished a "clean" mug out of the same water and filled it with beer. "I think you'd better slow down," he said, putting the beer in front of Bruce's neighbor before moving down the counter to take another order.

"Bartenders," the guy said in a disgusted tone, turning toward Bruce. "What do they know about anything?"

With a shock Bruce realized that the drunk next to him was the same blond guy he'd seen in the film library. He was wearing khakis and a light purple polo shirt, as if he'd dressed for better things, but his pants were wrinkled and stained with spilled beer. His equally damp polo had come untucked in back. *Who is this guy again?* Bruce wondered, racking his brain. But to his embarrassment, he still couldn't come up with a name.

"I mean, after all," Mr. Blond continued, "are

they here to serve drinks? Or to be people's mothers?"

"Serve drinks," Bruce muttered, turning away. The last thing he needed was to spend the night drinking with someone who reminded him of screenplays and Professor Gordon. *Oh, well, who cares,* Bruce thought, picking up his mug. *Down the hatch.*

Bruce drained off half the beer in one gulp. It wasn't cold enough, and water from the wet mug had diluted it in an unappetizing way. Before he could really taste it, Bruce tossed down the rest and raised a finger to signal the bartender for another.

"Here," Bruce's new drinking buddy offered, pushing his own fresh beer toward Bruce. "You've got some catching up to do."

Bruce looked askance at the mug, wondering if Mr. Blond had drunk out of it, but in the end he grabbed it and chugged the beer down even faster than before. He *did* have some catching up to do. He slammed the empty mug down hard on the bar and signaled impatiently for the bartender. The man eventually made his way down the counter, setting up new beers for the two of them before moving off again.

"Women!" Mr. Blond bellowed suddenly, apropos of nothing. He waved his full mug in front of him for emphasis.

"Tell me about it," Bruce agreed, wincing. How many beers was it going to take to get Lila out of his mind? He slumped over and sucked at the foam of his third beer without lifting the mug.

"You wouldn't believe the night I've had," Mr. Blond continued. "I met this fantastic girl—rich and beautiful, absolutely perfect. Everything was going great. Then tonight she *dumped* me—just like that. She told me she's seeing someone else! Can you believe it?"

Bruce picked up his beer and powered it down without answering. The guy had hit a nerve.

"It sounds like this other boyfriend of hers is a major jerk," Mr. Blond grumbled. "They had some kind of fight or something—I don't know. But now she says she loves him, so it's over. I've never been dumped before in my *life*."

"That's tough," Bruce commiserated, barely listening.

Mr. Blond nodded sadly and slurped at his beer. "The thing is, we would have been so perfect together. Like I said, she's rich—just like me."

Bruce flicked a look of ill-concealed disgust at his drinking partner. After all, Bruce was pretty well-off himself, but he didn't go around announcing it in divey bars. But Mr. Blond didn't seem to notice Bruce's expression at all.

"Do you know how hard it is to find a rich,

beautiful woman that wants anything to do with you?" Mr. Blond demanded, his brown eyes swimming in a sea of red.

"Uh, yeah, actually," Bruce admitted, signaling for another beer and wishing intensely that the guy would get off the subject of rich and beautiful women.

"Of course, tonight was nothing compared to what I've been through," Mr. Blond said. "The police found my last girlfriend dead."

"Dead?" Bruce repeated loudly, putting down his mug. "How did she die?"

"Suicide. What a laugh." The guy took several huge gulps of beer, shuddering as he swallowed.

Bruce didn't see anything funny about it. "I don't get it," he said flatly.

"Yeah. Neither did the police."

There was something about the way Mr. Blond spoke that put Bruce suddenly on his guard. "So . . . what are you saying? You don't think it was suicide?"

"I *know* it wasn't suicide. It was murder. Plain and simple."

"Did you tell that to the police?"

"Of *course* I didn't tell it to the police!" Mr. Blond exploded. "Do you think I'm stupid? Do you think I want . . ." He trailed off abruptly, as if he'd suddenly realized where he was and what he was saying. "Never mind," he muttered, turning his attention back to his beer. "It doesn't matter."

Bruce was stunned. At the very least, this guy knew something about a murder. At worst, he'd committed it himself. The possibility made Bruce's stomach tighten. "So who was this girl-friend of yours anyway?" Bruce asked, angling for clues. "What was her name?"

Mr. Blond snapped up straight, glanced around the room, and slid unsteadily off his barstool. "Forget everything I just said," he said urgently. "I—I shouldn't have opened my mouth." He regarded Bruce through beer-glazed eyes a moment longer, then pushed off into the crowd. Bruce kept an eye on him until he made his way out the front doors.

"Hey!" the bartender protested from across the bar. "Your friend didn't pay his tab."

Bruce fished a couple of twenties out of his wallet and threw them onto the wet, sticky bar with a shrug. *Some rich guy* he *turned out to be,* he thought, ordering another beer when the bartender took his cash.

The drink arrived and Bruce sipped at it slowly, the noise and pandemonium in the bar filtered out by the increasing alcohol haze in his brain. All he was really aware of anymore was the beer in front of him and the stool underneath him. And Mr. Blond . . .

Bruce cursed himself silently for not asking his name. The guy's story sounded awfully suspicious. But how could he report him to the police when he didn't even know who he was?

I'll keep an eye on him myself, Bruce decided as he swirled the dregs of his beer around in the mug. *I can always find out who he is in class next week.*

Jessica sailed through the Blue Lagoon's double doors, feeling extremely sophisticated. If her blow-dryer hadn't quit on her five minutes into its job she might have made it on time, but that certainly hadn't been *her* fault.

"Why are you doing this to me?" she'd screeched at the sputtering dryer. "Don't you know I have places to *go?*" But the dryer had refused to cooperate, and Jessica had been forced to beg up and down the hall for a loaner. It was all for the best, though. Shiny and loose, Jessica's perfectly styled hair brushed her denim-jacketed shoulders as she made her way toward the back of the bar, where Steven had said he and his friends liked to sit.

Of course, the blow-dryer disaster had been nothing compared to the shock of discovering that the whole ordeal had taken its toll on her new pink nail polish. "No, no, *no!*" she'd exclaimed in horrified disbelief. "This stuff is supposed to last a *week!*" She could have taken off the chipped polish and left her nails bare, but she was meeting *law-school* guys. No, the situation had demanded an emergency manicure.

Jessica held one hand in front of her in the crowded bar to admire the results of her polishing efforts, then tossed her silky hair. *Steven and his friends can wait an extra hour for this kind of perfection,* she reassured herself.

But when she got to the back of the bar, Jessica didn't see a single person she recognized. Where could they be? She scanned the crowd anxiously, looking for her brother. Instead her gaze drifted toward a grimy old art deco wall clock. It was almost nine.

"*We're only staying until eight-thirty,*" she could hear Steven saying as she mentally replayed their phone conversation. "*We're just going for a round or two, so don't be late 'cause we're not hanging around.* Jessica groaned loudly. Steven was actually *serious* about that?

Chewing her lip with annoyance, she turned and started walking back through the bar. It was a pretty ratty place, but the lively crowd of college students made it seem safe. Still, Jessica was glad she'd decided on faded jeans and a white halter top under her denim jacket——it obviously wasn't the kind of place you wanted to be dressed up in. The distinctive smell of spilled beer mixed with the odors of cigarette smoke and stale cooking oil in an overpowering reek that made her suddenly happy to be heading outside.

"Jessica!" a male voice rang out from

somewhere behind her. "Jessica! Over here!"

So they waited for me after all! Jessica cheered silently, stopping and turning slowly so that Steven's friends could experience the full impact of her gorgeousness. "Jessica!" the voice called again, and a dark-haired guy at the bar stood up to wave her over. Jessica sighed, disappointed. It wasn't Steven and his cute future lawyers—it was only Bruce Patman.

"What do you want, Bruce?" she asked after she'd pushed her way over to the empty barstool next to him.

"Whadda I *want?*" he repeated, looking injured. "I thought you might wanna drink with me, thass all." He patted the still-empty barstool. "Have a seat . . . I'm buyin'."

Jessica remained standing. "You know I don't drink, Bruce."

"S'have a ginger ale, fer cryin' out loud," he slurred. "Just siddown. Please."

Jessica hesitated, then hoisted herself up onto the barstool, wondering if he had driven there and, if so, how he was getting home. Jessica couldn't imagine Bruce driving his precious Porsche drunk, and she couldn't imagine anyone else being allowed to touch it either.

"Are you here by yourself?" she asked as Bruce shouted out an order for a beer and a soda.

Bruce bobbed his head. "Yup. All by myself,"

87

he confirmed. "With only Jessica Wakefield t'keep me comp'ny."

Jessica bristled.

"The *fab-lus* Jessica Wakefield," Bruce amended wobbily, slurping at his fresh beer the bartender had just put down. "Fab-lus . . ." He trailed off, as if he'd forgotten what he'd been saying.

"I think you've had a few too many," Jessica observed, pushing her untouched ginger ale down the counter. There was something floating in the glass that she didn't want to examine too closely. "You should go home."

"No," Bruce argued. "No, the problem is I've had a few too few. You wouldn't believe whadda horrible day I've had."

"And this is your way of dealing with it?" Jessica asked, disgusted.

Bruce shrugged, and for a moment the guard fell down in his blue eyes, revealing the pain beneath. "A lotta people deal with it this way."

"Did you and Lila have another fight?"

"I only wish," Bruce replied. "Y'see, I'd have to know where she is in order to fight with her. All *I* know is that she's out with some other guy."

Jessica's eyebrows flew up in surprise. *Lila cheating? How juicy!* she thought, settling into her barstool more comfortably. "I'm sure you're wrong, Bruce," she said in a way designed to invite him to reveal more.

"I'm not wrong," he said grimly. "Some guy named Marcus. Thass all I know."

Marcus . . . Marcus . . . Jessica searched through her mental Rolodex, but the name remained totally unfamiliar. "I've never heard Lila mention anyone named Marcus," she said truthfully.

Bruce brightened a little, then slumped again. "He sent her roses—thass all I know."

Roses? How romantic! Jessica's eyebrows creased. *I can't believe she never mentioned this guy to me. Some friend she is!*

"It's probably nothing," Jessica offered, still fishing for information. "For one thing, I doubt he's as handsome as you are." She held down a gag. *That'd better pay off,* she prayed.

"Lila's neighbor called him a total babe."

Bingo, she thought, pleased with her powers of persuasion. This fascinating turn of events was making missing Steven and his friends all seem worthwhile. *I can't wait to catch up with Lila and pump her for every detail.* In the meantime, though, she was stuck with clueless Bruce, who was getting drunker by the second.

"Come on, Bruce," she said, getting off her stool and pulling on his elbow. "We're leaving."

"Where-er-ee going?" he slurred, not uncooperatively. He peeled some bills off the stack in his wallet and tossed them onto the counter. "Your place?"

"You wish!" Jessica snorted derisively. "I'm taking you home to make sure you actually get there, that's all."

"How sweet," Bruce swooned, following her through the bar. "Yer so sweet."

Jessica felt a hand stroke her hair from behind, and she swatted it away. "I'm not that sweet," she warned over her shoulder. "Keep your hands to yourself, if you know what's good for you." She pushed through the double doors and found herself out on the sidewalk, Bruce right beside her. "Where's your Porsche?" she asked.

"At home. I walked here."

Jessica sighed with impatience and irritation. Not only was she going to have to walk him all the way to his apartment, but she'd also have to call for a cab to take her back to campus. No way was she covering that distance alone at night. "All right, then," she snapped. "Start walking."

Bruce took a few unsteady steps in the direction of his building, then spun around suddenly and began walking surprisingly quickly in the opposite direction.

"Where are you going?" Jessica demanded, following him. "You're going the wrong way."

"No, I'm not," Bruce responded, sounding a little more cheerful. "I juss remembered that Jack Johnson's havin' a birthday party tonight. S'probably just gettin' started."

Jessica groaned. Jack Johnson was a total jerk of a Sigma—even most of his fraternity brothers didn't like him. Jessica had known about the party, of course, but the likelihood of her going to it ranked right up there with the likelihood of her accidentally discovering a cure for cancer. "I'm *not* going to Jack Johnson's party," she said, hanging back on the sidewalk.

"C'mon, Jessica!" Bruce insisted, tripping over his own feet as he turned back and grabbed her by the arm. "It'll be fun."

"The guy has to throw his own birthday party. *That* ought to tell you something," she grumbled, but in the end she let herself be led. At least Jack's place wasn't far from Dickenson Hall. She could always ditch Bruce at the party and go home.

Lila hung up the phone with tears of worry and frustration in her eyes. She'd been trying to call Bruce ever since the taxi had brought her home from her aborted date with Marcus, but Bruce wasn't answering his telephone. As much as she wanted to say something—anything—that might get him to pick up or call her back, Lila hadn't left any messages. She didn't want to make up with him over a stupid answering machine.

"Where are you, Bruce?" she murmured out

loud, wiping at her wet eyes. It was late now, after midnight, and still he didn't answer. Was he home? Did he know it was her calling? *I guess he just doesn't want to talk to me,* she thought, her heart sinking even deeper.

Lila looked across the bedroom to her dresser, where Marcus's dozen roses seemed to glare at her like the twelve members of an accusing jury. She was sure now that she'd completely overreacted in taking a taxi home from the movies. Marcus had had a right to be upset at the way he'd been treated—it didn't make him *dangerous*. But instead of reassuring her, the knowledge only made her feel worse. Now she was guilty of hurting Marcus as well as betraying Bruce.

Pulling her blue silk bathrobe more tightly around her, Lila regarded Marcus's roses a moment longer before she made up her mind. The roses were going in the trash, and so was the new bouquet he had brought her earlier that evening. It was a terrible waste, but it was the only way to erase Marcus from her life and start fresh with Bruce.

Sticking her head out the front door to make sure no one was around, Lila ran outside in her bathrobe, juggling both bundles of flowers in her arms. She wrestled the heavy lid of the Dumpster open, dropped the flowers into its smelly depths, then let the cover drop with a resounding clang.

There. It was over.

Lila ran back into her cozy apartment and locked the door behind her again. "It never happened," she announced to the empty room. "I never even *met* Marcus Stanton."

If only she could believe that.

"Aw, you gotta come in, Jessica," Bruce begged as he leaned on Jack Johnson's front door buzzer.

Jessica rolled her eyes. "No, I *don't* 'gotta come in,'" she insisted, hearing the lame music blaring from inside the run-down duplex and what sounded like splashing from a swimming pool in the back.

"All yer friends are gonna be here."

"Puh-leeze!" Jessica gave him her most skeptical look. All *her* friends would be avoiding this party on principle—the principle of not being seen within fifty feet of Jack Johnson. Before she could say no, however, the door burst open and Jack was standing before them.

"Patman!" he exclaimed. "Come on in, dude! Who's the babe?"

Jessica winced. Jack knew perfectly well who she was. He was always such a pig.

Bruce grabbed her by the elbow and blew by Jack into the jam-packed living room. The place was standing room only and, to Jessica's surprise, there were quite a few people she recognized there after all. Most of the Sigmas had turned out to support their fraternity brother. The music was so loud, she could barely hear her heartbeat, and the air was close and hot. "Let's find the keg," Bruce yelled in her ear, dragging her in the direction of the backyard.

Outside was just slightly better. Jack's backyard was hideously ugly and composed completely of concrete—pool, patio, and block wall—but at least the air was fresher. Bruce spotted the keg over by the wall and headed right for it.

"You've had enough, Bruce," Jessica reminded him, following close behind.

"Jussa li'l one," he promised. "I got thirssy walkin' over here." He pumped the keg and held the foaming, sputtering nozzle down into a paper cup he'd grabbed off a stack wedged between the keg and the barrel full of ice it sat in. "Sure you doan wanna beer?"

She glared at Bruce fiercely, hands on her hips.

"All *right!*" he said defensively. "I'm only havin' one."

But it wasn't only one. It was more like one after another. Jessica fumed as Bruce drank beer after beer, leaving her standing ignored in the shadows at the edge of the patio. Jack's mostly male guests streamed steadily in and out of the house to get beers for themselves, many of them taking advantage of the opportunity to leer at Jessica, while Bruce remained glued to the keg. Jessica filled the long, boring minutes imagining ways to get even with him. But at the same time she realized that ditching him when he was in that state seemed a little *too* harsh a punishment. His eyes were glazed, his speech was thick, and he swayed where he stood. He'd never find his way back to his apartment.

"Hey, foxy lady," breathed a voice in her ear, accompanied by a stench of beer and onions. As she flinched away from the speaker someone pinched her behind from the other side.

"Ugh! You *losers!*" Jessica raged, wheeling to face the drunken frat boys on either side of her. "You're *disgusting!*"

Onion Breath laughed—it was Jack Johnson, naturally. "Take it easy, Jessica. It was just a little joke."

"Yeah," agreed the total stranger who stood on the side where she had been pinched. "Not that I wouldn't like to do it again," he added with a wink he apparently thought was sexy.

Jessica took a deep breath and slapped his drunken face hard.

"Hey!" he protested. Jack burst out laughing.

Jessica had her arm cocked back to slap Jack next when someone grabbed her wrist. "Whass goin' on here?" Bruce demanded from behind her, still holding on to Jessica's wrist—probably to keep himself upright.

"Your *friends,*" Jessica spat, "are *slime.*"

"Ah, lighten up, Jessica," Jack said. "You act like no one's ever pinched your butt before."

Jessica stiffened and wrested her arm out of Bruce's grip. Before she could act, however, Bruce grabbed Jack by the front of his shirt, lifting him right up off the ground. "Apologize to Jessica," he demanded, sounding surprisingly sober all of a sudden.

"Come on, buddy . . . ," Jack began. His weaselly friend skulked off the patio and ran back into the crowd.

"Apologize," Bruce repeated, lifting Jack higher.

"I'm sorry, Jessica," Jack said. "Jeez! Now put me down, Patman."

Bruce let go so quickly and unexpectedly that Jack's knees buckled when his feet hit the pavement. He recovered quickly and took off into the house.

"I'm leaving," Jessica announced indignantly. "Are you coming or not?" Without waiting for an answer, she stepped back into the living room and pushed her way through the crowd to the front door. She was halfway down the front walkway before Bruce caught up.

"Hey, wait for me!" he said as he drew up beside her. They both turned down the sidewalk in the direction of Dickenson Hall. "Whassa big hurry?"

Jessica shot him a poisonous look.

"Oh, that. Well, I saved you, didn't I?" He trotted along at her side, his balance so impaired that Jessica was tempted to call him the Leaning Tower of Patman.

"My hero," Jessica sneered. "If it weren't for you, I never would have been there in the first place."

Bruce seemed to make an attempt to ponder that statement, but the effort was obviously too much for him. "So where are we going now?" he managed.

"*I'm* going home," Jessica informed him. "You can go wherever you like." Her dorm had come into view—in another minute she'd be safely inside.

"I'll walk you home," Bruce offered.

Jessica silently pointed to the sign that read Dickenson Hall, rolled her eyes, and stormed through the front doors, making directly for the stairs to room 28. She'd had all she wanted to see of Bruce Patman for a very long time, but unfortunately she could hear stumbling footsteps behind her, following her all the way up to her dorm-room door. With a sigh Jessica unlocked the door and whirled around to face Bruce for what she hoped would be the last time that night.

"I'm home," she said shortly. "You can go now."

"OK," he agreed, grabbing both sides of the doorframe for support.

"I'm shutting the door now, Bruce. Let go."

Bruce nodded and let go of the doorframe. For a second he stood in her doorway unsupported, then his eyes rolled back into his head and his knees gave out underneath him. He toppled into her room like a felled tree, passed out cold on the thin institutional carpeting.

"Bruce! Bruce, wake up!" Jessica demanded, lifting his head off the floor and slapping his cheeks insistently.

"Lila," Bruce moaned. "Give ussa li'l kiss."

"Ugh!" Jessica exclaimed, dropping Bruce's head back onto the floor, where it landed with a thud that didn't seem to disturb him in the least. "When will this night be *over*?"

Chapter Six

This must be how it feels to get hit by an eighteen-wheeler, Bruce thought. Somewhere in the back of his head he heard a buzzing sound that was either a blow-dryer or his own muddled brain. Bruce held himself absolutely motionless, listening. Maybe it was only his ears ringing. Whatever it was, it seemed to get louder and softer in time with his pulse.

If still I have a pulse, then I must be alive, Bruce reasoned, but the way he felt made it hard to be sure. He'd never been so hung over in his life.

Groaning, Bruce forced open his eyes, squinting in pain as they were assaulted by blinding sunlight. He was lying on his back beside an open window, but where? It didn't get this bright in his apartment. He glanced down and saw an unfamiliar blanket covering the lower half of his still-clothed body. This wasn't his bed! Where *was* he?

With an enormous effort Bruce rose into a sitting position. The room reeled around him, and his head felt like it was about to implode. The contents of his stomach rose up into his throat. Bruce gagged at the taste of stale beer and barely managed to keep from puking.

"Good morning, sunshine," chirped a female voice to his right.

Fighting the stabbing pain at his temples, Bruce turned his head far enough to see Jessica Wakefield sitting on the twin bed next to his. It was all he could do to keep from groaning again—he was in no mood to trade insults with Jessica this morning.

"Wait a minute—what are *you* doing here?" Bruce asked in amazement.

Jessica raised her eyebrows. "I live here."

What! Bruce blinked repeatedly to clear the film floating over his eyes, then forced himself to focus on the details of the room. His stomach lurched again as the horror of his situation finally dawned on him. He was in the Wakefield twins' dorm room—in one of their beds!

Oh, man, what happened last night? he asked himself, desperately trying to think. His mind raced, but nothing came back. He remembered going to the Blue Lagoon and drinking with that weird Mr. Blond. After a moment's strain he remembered running into Jessica there. But everything after that was hazy.

"How did I get here?" he asked, closing his eyes against the glare and pulling the covers up higher as he lay back down.

"You walked," said Jessica. "Don't you remember?"

"I don't remember anything."

"Anything?"

"I remember the Blue Lagoon, and that's about it," Bruce admitted.

"You don't remember going to that sleaze Jack Johnson's party?"

"We went to Johnson's party?" Bruce repeated, shocked. "I don't even like the guy."

"That's good." Jessica giggled. "Because I don't think he likes you anymore either. The way you acted, I doubt you'll be invited to his next big soiree." From the amused tone of her voice Bruce could only assume he'd made a fool of himself somehow.

"So what did we do after the party?" he asked reluctantly. He hated to give Jessica the thrill of telling him, but how else was he going to find out?

Jessica smiled—a slow, incredulous smile. "We came back here. You really don't remember?"

"I already said I didn't," he growled irritably. "What did we come *here* for? Where's Elizabeth?"

"Elizabeth's out of town."

"Out of town where?"

"L.A. She and her journalism class have been gone all week." Jessica raised her eyebrows at him suggestively. "It's just you and me."

"You mean . . . we're *alone* here?" Bruce gasped.

"All alone," Jessica confirmed.

"But . . . but . . . I spent the night here?"

"You certainly did."

"Oh no," Bruce groaned. What would happen when word got out that he and Jessica had spent the night in the same room? "Perfect," he said sarcastically.

"Funny," Jessica purred, moving to sit on his bed and stroke his chest through the fabric of his shirt. "That's exactly what you said last night, lover boy."

Bruce's eyes flew open, only to see Jessica's blue-green ones staring directly into his. A sly, satisfied smile curved her lips.

"You can't mean . . . ? We didn't . . . ," Bruce stammered.

"Didn't what, sweetie? I think we did everything you could think of."

"Don't even *joke* about this, Jessica!" Bruce begged. "If Lila thinks we did *anything* together, I'm finished."

"You weren't worried about Lila last night," Jessica said with a little pout. "Anyway, isn't this better all the way around? Lila has a new boyfriend now and—"

"That guy's *not* her boyfriend!" Bruce shouted defensively. "*I'm* her boyfriend."

Jessica looked shocked. "I thought you were *my* boyfriend."

"*Your* boyfriend? Why would I be *your* boyfriend?"

"*Why?*" Jessica repeated, clearly stunned. "After everything that happened between us last night, you can still ask me that? Oh, sure, I guess you got what you wanted and now it's all over!"

"What I *wanted?*" Bruce repeated weakly. "Come on, Jessica, tell the truth. Nothing really happened. Right?"

"So *that's* going to be your story!" Jessica leaped up and glared down at him furiously. "I can't believe I trusted you! You said you *loved* me!"

"I said *what?*" Bruce squeaked.

"I suppose you want to take it all back now!" Jessica sneered confrontationally. "Do you always lie when you get between the sheets?"

"What do you mean, 'between the sheets'?" Bruce asked, blood pounding in his ears. "There's hardly enough room in this bed for *me*, let alone anyone else."

Jessica froze, as if taken by surprise, and the scowl faded slowly from her face. A moment later she smiled, then giggled. Bruce took in her expression and breathed an enormous sigh of relief. *Gotcha,* he thought triumphantly. *So you have been yanking my chain all along—*

"Oh, Bruce," Jessica said, still giggling. "It was a pretty tight squeeze, but we managed. If you only knew how silly you looked—"

"Enough!" Bruce shouted, wishing he could

silence both Jessica Wakefield and the pounding roar in his ears. So Jessica *wasn't* kidding? He'd cheated on the woman he loved with her best friend!

I've committed the worst romantic crime there is without even knowing it, he realized, his heart sinking to the floor. *Now I'll never get Lila back. I could forgive her for going out with another guy last night, but she'll never, ever forgive me for this.*

"I'm sorry, Lila," Bruce moaned.

Jessica laughed and winked conspiratorially. "Hey, I won't tell Lila if you don't."

Lila walked up the Dickenson Hall stairs, exhausted from worry. She was sure that Bruce was missing. Calling him all night and getting nothing but his machine was one thing, but going to his apartment first thing in the morning and discovering that it was as silent as a tomb— with the Porsche still parked in the garage—was another matter completely.

"I just know he hates me now," she fretted, nervously twisting a strand of brown hair around her finger as she walked. "He knows about the roses, after all. When I find him, I'll just admit that I made a big mistake, that's all."

Wild thoughts raced through Lila's brain now as she approached room 28. What if something bad had happened to him? Maybe he'd been attacked somewhere and left unconscious. Maybe he had been out all night with another woman to get back at her.

"Get a grip, Lila," she ordered herself under her breath. "Your imagination is running away with you. Once you talk to Jessica, she'll help you get it all straightened out. Maybe she'll even know where Bruce is." She composed herself for a moment, feeling semirelieved already. Then she knocked.

"Come in," Jessica sang out. "It's open."

Jessica wasn't exactly a morning person, and Lila cocked an eyebrow in surprise at her cheerful tone. "*You're* awfully happy this morning," Lila remarked, turning the doorknob and stepping into the room. A second later she froze in her tracks, stunned by the sight that met her eyes. Bruce was lying in bed with the covers pulled up to his chin, looking groggy and disheveled. Beside him sat Jessica, an enormous smile on her wide-awake face.

"Bruce!" Lila gasped.

"Lila! I can explain!" Bruce exclaimed guiltily, struggling to sit up.

Lila stared at him in disbelief, her mind reeling. "I doubt that very much!"

"No, we really can—" Jessica began, her expression clouding up with apparent concern.

Lila stared down her best friend as seething-hot rage coursed madly through her veins. "Don't even *talk* to me! You . . . you backstabbing *witch!*" The thought of Bruce and her now ex–best friend together made Lila feel physically ill. "How *dare* you?" she screamed. "*Both* of you!"

"No, Lila! It's not like that," Bruce whimpered pitifully. "Nothing happened."

Lila could tell just by looking at him that he was lying. He wasn't even man enough to confess when he was caught red-handed. He was pathetic!

"Don't even try, Bruce," she spat, looking from him to Jessica. "I could *kill* you right now."

"Lila, it's really not what you think—" Jessica began, looking every bit as guilty as Bruce.

"Shut up!" Lila screamed, tears springing to her eyes. "I *hate* you! I hate you *both!*"

"Wait! Lila!" they protested in unison, but she was already out the door, running as fast as she could. Tears streamed down her face as Lila sped blindly down the stairwell. She'd never speak to Bruce Patman again for as long as she lived. Never, never, *never*. And Jessica! How could she have done something so low after all their years as best friends? She never wanted to speak to her again either.

Lila burst through the main doors of Dickenson Hall and kept on running. *No, that's not true,* Lila realized through her rage, *I'd like to talk to her one last time. I'll give her a piece of my mind that she'll never forget!*

At the thought the tears came faster, and Lila suddenly realized that she had no idea where she was running. And when she stopped in the middle of the quad and tried to get her bearings back, a tiny voice crept into her head—a voice that sounded much like her own.

If you hadn't gone out with Marcus, none of this would have happened.

Lila put her head in her hands and dropped to the ground, sobbing.

"I'm not kidding, Jessica. Let me up right now!" Bruce insisted weakly, struggling beneath the covers. "I have to catch Lila!" He tried to push Jessica off the edge of the bed, but he was too hung over to do it.

"Oh yeah. You really look like you're in a condition to go running after her," Jessica said sarcastically. "You can't even sit up. Now shut up and let me think!"

Jessica could still barely believe that her harmless little joke on Bruce had turned so tragically ugly. After the horrible night he'd put her through, she'd figured he had a little payback coming. Making him believe that the two of them had spent a wild, passionate night together had been sweet revenge while it lasted. She'd never intended to let things go far enough to hurt Lila, though, and now it was too late.

"I can't believe this is happening," Bruce

moaned, still struggling to get out of bed. "Why did I even come here with you? How could I have been so *stupid?*"

"Thanks very much," Jessica retorted.

"You know what I mean, Jessica," Bruce returned. "How could we have done this to Lila? I have to find her and apologize!"

"Will you relax?" Jessica pushed him back down on the bed easily with the fingers of one hand. "You *are* stupid, Bruce. But you aren't unfaithful. I was having a little fun with you, that's all."

"Fun?" he echoed blankly.

"When I ran into you at the Blue Lagoon, you were already drunk. I only went to that stupid party with you because I didn't think you'd make it home by yourself. You got even drunker at Jack's, followed me back to my room, and passed out cold. When I went to bed, you were still snoring on the floor. I guess you woke up and climbed into Liz's bed sometime during the night." Jessica watched Bruce's numbed face impatiently as he seemed to struggle to make sense of what she was saying.

"Then, uh, nothing happened?"

Jessica snorted. "Like I'd let you near me."

"Thank goodness!" Bruce exploded. "Oh, wow. What a relief!" He lay back on the pillow and closed his eyes again.

In the plain sunlight streaming through the window, Jessica noticed that Bruce's eyelids looked almost translucent. In fact, his whole face was deathly pale, and dark, etched circles extended down from the inside corners of his eyes. For someone so vain, he looked terrible.

"Hey, are you feeling OK?" she asked. "You don't look so hot."

Bruce opened his eyes. They seemed glassy, unfocused. "I've never been this hung over before," he admitted. "I feel like hell. No thanks to you."

"Are you going to throw up?" she asked, concerned for Elizabeth's bedspread. "Should I bring you a wastebasket or something?"

"No," Bruce said, irritated. "I have to *get* up and find Lila." But Bruce didn't move.

"So are you getting up or what?"

"I . . . I . . . in a minute," Bruce said, looking totally defeated. His hands clutched the edge of the blanket convulsively, as if he were really in pain.

Jessica stared down at him with surprise. All this helplessness certainly wasn't in keeping with his usual macho image. *Maybe I should call a doctor*, she thought worriedly, but a moment later she brushed the idea aside. It was only a hangover, and he'd certainly earned it.

"Well, if you want my advice, you'll take a shower before you go after Lila," Jessica told him, wrinkling her nose for emphasis. "Besides, Lila will never talk to you unless I find her first and explain things."

"I'd rather explain them myself," he insisted, not opening his sunken eyes.

"No doubt, but you know Lila won't believe a word you say if I don't set her straight."

Bruce groaned. "Yeah . . . I guess you're right."

"Listen, you take it easy a few more minutes, then go home and clean yourself up. I'll find Lila and smooth everything over."

"You promise?"

"She's my friend too, Bruce," Jessica reminded him indignantly. "I don't want her running around thinking I'm a backstabber any more than you do."

Bruce nodded and rolled over to face the wall. "Just a couple more minutes," he said, his voice drifting groggily. "And then I'll get up."

"Yeah, well, don't sleep *too* late. It's Thursday, remember? The Beringer dedication?"

"Ugh. That's the last . . . thing on my mind . . . right now. . . ." He trailed off and began snoring in big, roaring gasps.

Jessica clucked her tongue at the disgusting sight. "Just don't drool on Liz's sheets," she grumbled before grabbing her backpack and sailing out the door.

Bruce awoke with a start. "Ugh . . . what time is it?" He sat up quickly, then nearly retched as the pain seized his head again. With a massive

110

effort of will he swung his legs out of Elizabeth's bed and stood unsteadily.

"I've got to get home," he said with a groan, checking the digital clock on Elizabeth's desk. It was eleven thirty-five. Jessica must have left hours before. "Jeez. How could I have fallen back asleep?"

At least he remembered where he was now and why. That was a big improvement from the last time he'd woken up in this room. *Still, I never should have* been *in this room in the first place,* he chastised himself, praying that Jessica had found Lila and gotten everything straightened out.

Stumbling in his cowboy boots, Bruce made his way to the door and out into the hall. Thursday classes were in session, and the hallway was mercifully empty. Gripping the top of his throbbing head with one hand, Bruce used the other to steady himself as he made his way down the stairs and out into the sunshine. The light stung his eyes and made the pain in his head more piercing, but Bruce had no choice but to drag himself to his apartment on foot. He was so tired that the half-mile trek felt more like an Olympic marathon.

Sweating and shaking, Bruce covered the final few feet to his front door and pulled out his keys with a trembling hand. They dropped to the ground, and as he bent to retrieve them he noticed a large plastic-foam cup on the floor next to his doormat. Under the cup was a folded sheet of notebook paper.

"What's this?" he muttered, grabbing the keys with one hand and the cup and paper with the other. Leaning against the door, Bruce struggled with the lock, sighing with immense relief when the door finally swung open.

"Home at last!" Bruce stumbled into his living room and flopped down on the couch, studying the things he had found on his doorstep. The oversize cup read The Java Joint in familiar, block letters, and he immediately recognized the aroma wafting from under the lid—the house brew, his favorite. Bruce unfolded the accompanying sheet of paper to find a cryptic note:

> Bruce, I think it's time you wake up and smell the coffee.
>
>   Li

It wasn't exactly a love letter, but at least she was still communicating with him. "Thank you, Jessica, for whatever you did," Bruce breathed, popping the white plastic lid off the coffee cup. "Maybe I'll forgive you for pulling that stunt in the first place." He held the coffee under his nose, taking in the rich, dark scent. It was barely warm—maybe it had been sitting on his doorstep for a while—but it still smelled delicious. He took a small swallow, then a big one. Gradually his head began to clear.

"Caffeine," he said out loud. "Why didn't *I* think of that?" By the time Bruce was finished, he felt significantly better. Not good, but better. He went into the kitchen and grabbed a bottle of aspirin out of the cupboard over the sink, taking three for good measure. Aspirin on an empty stomach seemed like a bad idea, so Bruce scrounged through his near empty fridge and rescued a piece of stale bread from between two petrified heels in a plastic bag. Bruce toasted it and ate it dry.

The bread didn't sit well, and for a second Bruce thought that everything—coffee, aspirin, and toast—was coming back up. He ran to the bathroom, his stomach heaving, and fell to his knees on the tile floor. The moment passed and his stomach settled down, but the race to the bathroom had left him dizzy and nauseous. He sat up with his back against the side of the bathtub, the porcelain cool through the cotton of his T-shirt. It felt so good that he wriggled around sideways and laid his cheek down on the smooth white rim of the tub.

Minutes passed. The room stopped spinning. And Bruce realized that what he needed was a shower. Still on the floor, Bruce kicked off his boots and pants, then pulled his T-shirt off over his head. The effort exhausted him and he shivered unhappily, naked on the cold tile floor. It was not one of the more dignified moments of his life, and he knew it.

"If I survive this hangover, I'll never, ever drink again," he vowed.

Chapter Seven

"Ah," Bruce sighed contentedly. Working up the strength to stand up in the shower had taken half an hour, but it was worth it. The steam worked its way deep into Bruce's lungs as the hot, revitalizing water cascaded over his head and shoulders. Shutting off the faucet with another, reluctant sigh, Bruce grabbed a clean, fluffy towel off the back of the shower door and dried himself. The room had finally stopped spinning, and his stomach seemed to have decided to keep the toast. Even so, he still felt horrible.

I wish I could just climb into bed and pull the covers over my head for the next twenty-four hours, he thought. The idea of sleeping off the hangover was so attractive that for a moment Bruce almost gave in. But it was impossible. No matter how bad he felt, he had to straighten things out with Lila. So instead of going back to bed, Bruce put on some clean clothes and headed for Lila's apartment.

We have a lot to talk about, Lila, he rehearsed mentally as he walked down the sidewalk. The distance between their apartments was a lot farther than Bruce would normally have chosen to travel by foot, but he didn't feel well enough to drive. *For starters, where you were last night. And with whom.*

Actually, the more he thought about it, the less Bruce relished having any such conversation. For one thing, even if Jessica had spoken to Lila, there were sure to be plenty of counteraccusations. Not only that, but if Lila had a serious new love interest, Bruce didn't want to know about it. On the other hand, they were going to have to get everything out in the open if they wanted to save their relationship, and Bruce *definitely* wanted to save their relationship.

I know I haven't been too great of a boyfriend the last few weeks, he tried again, setting his mind to the task of apologizing. *But I want to start over if you'll let me.* Bruce shook his head impatiently. *No! That sounds totally weak!*

If only he could concentrate, he'd come up with the right words to say, but he still felt lousy—in fact, he needed to sit down. Bruce glanced around for a place to rest but found only the sidewalk beneath his boots. He was actually considering sitting down on the concrete when suddenly it went out of focus and a loud buzzing erupted in his ears. Startled, Bruce shook his head in an attempt to clear his vision, but the motion made him dizzy. Silver spots floated around him like the flakes in a snow dome. The nausea was back— even worse than before—and a cold sweat broke out on his forehead. Bruce put a trembling hand to the skin on the back of his neck. It was on fire.

"What's happening?" Bruce whispered urgently. "What do I do?" He wanted to go home, but he knew he'd never make it; Lila's apartment was much closer.

Bruce imagined himself lying on Lila's pastel sofa with a cool cloth on his head and Lila fussing over him. It wasn't an unpleasant picture. *If I'm sick, she might even feel sorry for me,* he realized. *That'll make making up a lot easier.* Then in the evening, when his hangover receded, he'd take her out somewhere nice for dinner.

Bruce had taken a tentative step in the direction of Lila's apartment when he noticed something odd. The sidewalk seemed to be moving. Yes, it was rushing up to meet him! *He* was standing perfectly motionless, but the sidewalk . . .

Bruce's head hit the pavement with a dull, hollow thud. Then his entire world went black.

"Bruce! Bruce, can you hear me?"

Bruce heard the voice in a dim, vague kind of way through the buzzing in his ears.

117

"Bruce, try to open your eyes, please."

Ugh. Can't a guy get any sleep? he wondered, feeling someone squeezing his hand. With a massive effort he forced his eyes open. A woman he had never seen before stared down at him.

"Welcome back," she said. "How do you feel?"

Bruce considered the question with a muddled brain. "Like hell," he responded, his tongue thick and uncooperative.

"I'll bet," the woman agreed. "I'm Dr. Martin, by the way."

"Doctor?" Bruce repeated, alarmed. *Where am I?* He tried to sit up, but the doctor restrained him.

"You're in the hospital," she told him as if she had read his thoughts. "You passed out on the street, and someone called an ambulance—we got your information from your wallet. You hit your head pretty hard, so don't be surprised if it throbs a little."

Bruce tried to laugh, but it hurt too much. "I'm not sure I'll notice the difference. I've had hangovers before, but this is ridiculous."

The doctor seemed disturbed. "We did find traces of alcohol in your system. But I'm afraid your problem is *not* a hangover, Bruce, even though heavy drinking may have intensified the nausea."

Bruce shook his head, confused. The movement sent a shooting pain up into his eye sockets, making him grimace. "Of course it's a hangover," he said stubbornly. "I can't believe I was lame enough to fall down, but I had *way* too much to drink last night. It made me sick."

"That's not what made you sick," the doctor insisted quietly. The expression on her face was so serious that Bruce felt suddenly cold. "At least, that's not the problem anymore."

Bruce's uneasy attempt at laughter was once more aborted by pain. "You wouldn't say that if you'd seen me last night. Look, Dr. Martin, I feel like an idiot for passing out, and I'm sorry I wasted your time. Don't worry, I'll pay for everything."

This time Bruce managed to sit up before the doctor could stop him, getting his first good look at his surroundings. He saw that he was on a gurney in a cubicle walled off by green curtains. An empty IV bottle hanging from a chrome-plated rack was the only other furniture in the room.

"We put some fluids in you while you were unconscious," the doctor explained. "That ought to take care of the hangover. We also did some blood work."

"Blood work!" Bruce protested. "For a hangover? You've got to be kidding me." He swung his legs off the gurney, but the doctor spoke again before he could go any farther.

"I'm sorry, Bruce, but there's no delicate way to put this. You've been poisoned."

◆　　◆　　◆

Lila began singing along with the radio as she guided her sports car down the freeway, then stopped, annoyed with herself. What did she have to sing about? Her life was a total mess. She jabbed the station buttons on her stereo until she found a talk show.

"Once again, for you listeners who are just tuning in, our subject today is 'Good for the Goose, Good for the Gander,'" the DJ announced in a smarmy, insinuating tone. "So, all you cheatin' hearts out there, give us a call and give us the dirt. We want to know: Was it good for *you?*"

Lila snapped off the radio abruptly and let out an irate snarl. What kind of stupid subject was that? She barely noticed the sudden silence in the car; there was too much rattling around in her head. For one thing, she still hadn't spoken to Bruce. She'd expected him to come by her apartment after he'd read her note, but he hadn't even bothered to call her.

Well, he *can sit around wondering where* I *am this time,* she thought vindictively as she guided the car down the off-ramp toward Fowler Crest. Even though Lila was hardly in the celebrating mood, today was Mrs. Fowler's birthday; she and her parents were going to spend the afternoon together at their stately mansion before heading to Andre's, her mother's favorite restaurant, for dinner. If Bruce came looking for her later, he'd have no idea where she'd gone. The way things were going, he'd probably think she was out with another guy.

And that's just fine, she told herself, a small, bitter smile on her lips. He deserved to suffer. Briefly, guiltily, Lila remembered how that same feeling led her to accept a date with Marcus Stanton—but she quickly brushed it all aside. *That whole fiasco was Bruce's fault too,* she reasoned. *If Bruce had been a half-decent boyfriend, Marcus never would have had a chance.*

Lila took a few slow, deep breaths as the entrance to Fowler Crest came into view. It seemed like an eternity since she'd lived there and gone to Sweet Valley High. Lila had loathed Bruce Patman then.

"That's because I was *smarter* then," she muttered, a small chuckle escaping her lips as she remembered the little gift she left on Bruce's doorstep. "I sure hope he liked that coffee."

Bruce stared at the doctor in shock. *Poisoned?* Had he heard correctly? He opened his mouth to argue, but just as suddenly it all became clear. The doctor was pulling his leg, of course. If he wasn't still half comatose, he'd have gotten it right away. Dr. Martin must have found Lila's phone number in his wallet, and the two of them had come up with this little gag to make him think he was the title character in his own screenplay.

"Poisoned!" he chuckled, relieved. "Good one! You had me going there for a second. Lila told you to say that, I bet. Where is she?"

The doctor simply looked at him as if he were delirious.

"Oh, come on, Dr. Martin. It's a joke, right? She must have told you about my screenplay."

"I'm sorry, Bruce," the doctor replied, her voice tense and concerned, "but you're not making any sense. I'd never joke about something this serious."

Bruce rolled his eyes. Dr. Martin, if that was her real name, was one convincing actress, and Lila was probably listening through the curtain. OK—if they wanted an act, he'd give them one. "No, of course not. How long have I got, Doc?" he gasped, grabbing at his throat like a dying cowboy in a bad Western. "It's all getting so hazy," he added theatrically, swaying back and forth on the gurney and groping blindly in front of him. "So . . . hazy."

"Stop that right now!" Dr. Martin snapped, and Bruce stopped in an instant. She looked dead serious.

"Now *listen* to me, Bruce," she demanded. "There's no one here named Lila, and I haven't seen any screenplay. I've seen your lab results, though. You've got some kind of unusual poison in your bloodstream and *that's* what's making you sick."

"That can't be," Bruce scoffed. "Who'd want to

poison me? Your lab must have made a mistake. And anyway, I'm starting to feel better now."

Dr. Martin stepped closer and peered into Bruce's eyes for a long moment, then nodded as if satisfied. "The drugs we gave you for pain and vertigo are starting to take effect, but they won't last. And when they wear off, you're going to feel even worse."

Bruce had another smart remark on the tip of his tongue, but something about Dr. Martin's demeanor made him stop. Her expression was so earnest. It was almost as if . . .

It's true! The sudden realization jolted Bruce right down to his soul. Someone had actually *poisoned* him. *But that's not possible!* he assured himself. *Maybe I ate some bad food. Or maybe it's* alcohol *poisoning. . . .*

"This is important, Bruce," Dr. Martin urged. "You need to think back over everything you've had to eat or drink in the last twenty-four hours. Any clue you can give us to identify the toxin could help save your life."

Bruce looked up, startled. "Aren't you exaggerating a little?"

The doctor shook her head sadly. "I'm afraid not. That poison has already broken down to the point that we can't identify it without extensive testing. If we don't figure out what it is and find you an antidote, you have less than twenty-four hours to live."

"It's *fatal*? I'm going to *die*?"

The doctor put a reassuring hand on his shoulder. "Only if we don't find the antidote. But we have one of the finest labs in California, Bruce, and you're young and strong. It's entirely possible that . . ."

Bruce blocked Dr. Martin's voice out of his head. What did it matter that their lab was good or that he was young? Someone had *poisoned* him. His entire world had just folded in on top of him.

And only twenty-four hours left to live? The whole situation was too eerily familiar.

He had become *The Victim*.

"I have every technician in the lab working on identifying that poison, Bruce," Dr. Martin said, breaking into his thoughts. "But there are so many possibilities, and the tests take time."

Her words struck him like a bad déjà vu. Bruce had already known what she was going to say. He had already *written* what she was going to say.

"I have to find out who poisoned me," he said, his voice strange and foreign in his ears, as if he were reading for an audition.

Dr. Martin nodded. "I'm afraid that may be your best hope. If you could find the person who did this to you and find out exactly what was used, then I could definitely help you. Otherwise, well, we'll keep working in the lab. . . ." As she let the sentence trail off, Bruce shuddered involuntarily.

"You said less than twenty-four hours," he whispered. "How much less?"

"I can't say exactly. It depends—"

"Then guess!"

"Sometime before dawn tomorrow. Maybe a couple of hours either way."

Dawn. That was no time at all. Would he really be dead before dawn? The thought seemed unreal.

"I have to go," Bruce said, stumbling to his feet.

"Are you sure you're up to it?"

"What choice do I have?"

The doctor peered intently into his eyes, checked his pulse, then nodded. "At least take this," she urged, removing a beeper from her lab coat and pressing it into his hands. "If we come up with anything, I'll page you immediately."

Bruce nodded and clipped the beeper to the waistband of his jeans. Without another word, he pushed his way through the gauzy green curtains and out into the polished brightness of the hospital corridor, his legs numb beneath him. Hall after hall went by in a daze before he passed through the main lobby doors and onto the street.

He blinked in the sunshine, temporarily surprised that the world still looked so normal. His body felt as if it belonged to a stranger. Slowly, painfully, he headed down the sidewalk. But panic sank in as he realized that he didn't have time to stroll around. He could feel every second ticking away, and those ticks were growing faster. He had to move.

The concrete passed erratically beneath his boots as Bruce quickened his pace from a walk to a trot to a run. He knew what he had to do.

He had to find his killer.

Or die trying.

Chapter Eight

"Someone's got to help me!" Bruce yelled, bursting through the double glass doors of the Sweet Valley police station. "Now!"

"Please wait your turn in line, sir," the receptionist said calmly. "And then I'll be happy to help you."

"I don't have time to wait in line!" Bruce countered frantically, ignoring how every person waiting in line was staring at him as if he were out of his mind. "This isn't a missing bicycle we're talking about! It's murder!"

"Who's been murdered, sir?" the alarmed receptionist asked, reaching for the telephone on her desk.

"I have!" Bruce shouted.

Barely suppressed laughter rose up in the reception area, and Bruce realized too late that he should have just made something up. Anything would have been more believable than the truth.

"You seem very much alive to me, sir," the receptionist replied with a smirk. She took her hand away from the telephone and returned her attention to the forms on the counter in front of her. "Please wait your turn."

Bruce considered arguing further before he noticed the large, muscular guard on the other side of the reception area. Reluctantly Bruce took his place in line.

Shifting impatiently from one foot to the other, Bruce watched the minutes fly by on the institutional-style clock with a growing sense of dread. It seemed as if every precious tick of the second hand shaved an hour off his life. He could actually feel Dr. Martin's medication holding down the effects of the poison, but under that he could sense the poison itself, throbbing in his ears, tightening his stomach, revving his pulse erratically. Five minutes passed. Then ten. Then fifteen. Then it was finally his turn.

"My name is Bruce Patman, and I've been poisoned," he blurted out to the receptionist. "Dr. Martin over at the hospital will confirm that. The only way they can find an antidote is if you guys help me find the person who poisoned me. If we don't find out anything by dawn, I'm going to die."

The receptionist looked at him skeptically. "If you're so sick, then why aren't you still in the hospital?"

"Because they can't help me there! Now please, will you call a detective?"

"I will, but they'll want to check your story with the hospital first. What is Dr. Martin's first name?"

"I—I don't know," Bruce stammered, his stomach clenching even tighter. "There can't be that many Dr. Martins working emergency right now. Can't you just call the hospital and ask?"

The receptionist nodded vaguely and indicated a row of dilapidated green chairs against the far wall. "Have a seat, Mr. Patman. I'll let the detectives know you're waiting."

"I already waited!" Bruce protested loudly. "I need to see someone *now!*"

"It will only be another minute. Please take a seat."

Bruce hesitated, then dragged himself over to one of the chairs and sat down. It was literally killing him to wait, but he didn't have much choice. Still, he was relieved to sit down; the wait in line had taken its toll on his weakening legs and back. But a few minutes passed, then a few more, and still no detective came out into the lobby.

"What's the story?" he called impatiently to the receptionist. "What's going on?"

"They're all tied up, Mr. Patman. Someone will be with you in a minute."

"That's what you said fifteen minutes ago!" Bruce exploded, looking nervously at the clock.

He'd already been there over half an hour and he hadn't accomplished anything. He'd be just as close to finding his killer if he'd stayed in the hospital. *What did I really expect the police to do for me anyway?* Bruce wondered, rising to his feet and heading for the door. *They weren't any help in my screenplay either. And Professor Gordon thought that was unrealistic!*

"Bruce Patman," called a gravelly male voice, stopping Bruce in his tracks. "Detective Frank Warren. I'll see you now."

"Finally!" Bruce exclaimed. "I was just leaving."

Detective Warren shrugged apologetically. "Frankly, Mr. Patman, we didn't believe your story. But I've spoken with your doctor, and everything checks out. Come back to my office and I'll help you."

Bruce followed the detective to the back of the police station and into a small, private office.

"Have a seat," Detective Warren offered, closing the door behind them and pouring some coffee into a thick paper cup. "Here," he said, extending it to Bruce. "I thought maybe you could use this."

Bruce stared at the cup, dumbfounded. Had everyone gone insane? He was dying, and the police wanted to take time out for a coffee break! He was just about to refuse when he caught a whiff of the aroma. *Not as good as what Lila brought me,* he thought, *but it'll do.*

"Thanks," he mumbled, taking the hot cup from the detective's hand and sipping at it gratefully.

The detective poured more coffee into an old chipped mug and seated himself across the table. "I have your preliminary report here from the desk clerk, but we're going to need a lot more information if we're going to catch the person who did this to you. I need names, addresses, relationships. Is there anyone you can think of who would want to kill you?"

"Only my girlfriend," Bruce said wryly, remembering Lila's outraged face when she found him in Jessica's room. "No, that was a joke!" he added quickly as Detective Warren made a note. "I honestly can't think of anyone. No one at all."

"Well, who have you spent time with in the last twenty-four hours?" the detective asked, leaning back in his chair.

Bruce struggled to remember. The last twenty-four hours were a major blur. The only person who could possibly retrace Bruce's steps was Jessica.

"Well, I, uh, went to a bar," Bruce began. "The Blue Lagoon. I had a few too many beers, then I ran into Jessica."

"Jessica?"

"Jessica Wakefield. Unfortunately I barely remember anything after that. She told me we went to a party, and then I apparently passed out at her place."

"This Jessica Wakefield," the detective said, leaning forward. "Have you known her long?"

"Oh, I know what you're thinking," Bruce said hurriedly. "It wasn't Jessica."

"How do you know?"

Bruce groaned internally. Only five minutes into the questioning, and already the police were off track! "I just know, all right?"

Detective Warren's eyebrows went up. "You never know," he offered, writing something on a long form in triplicate.

Maybe he's right, Bruce wondered. *She did pull that trick on me this morning. Who's to say she wouldn't try to pull another "innocent" prank—and have that one backfire too?*

"Here," the detective said, pushing the form across the table. "I want you to fill this out as completely as possible."

Bruce looked down at the paper in front of him, his chest heaving. At the top of the form was Jessica's name, and beneath that were about fifty blanks that needed to be filled in: her age, address, physical description, family members, criminal record . . . "I can't fill this out!"

"Why not?" asked the detective.

"Because it's a waste of time! Jessica didn't do it. It could have been anyone else. It could have been that weirdo from my film class, for all I know."

"What weirdo?" the detective asked patiently,

his pencil poised over another, identical form.

In a flash Bruce realized how the rest of the interview would unfold. The pot of coffee, the pile of paperwork . . . by the time the police got around to actually *looking* for anyone, Bruce would already be dead.

Dead.

"I don't have time for this," Bruce said, bolting up from his chair in a panic. His legs wobbled beneath him. "I have to go."

"Go where?" Detective Warren protested. "I'm trying to help you."

"No time," Bruce repeated, walking out the office door and back through the station. No one even tried to stop him as he made his way quickly back out to the street.

The sun was still hot overhead, but it was lower in the sky now—so much time had already been lost. Bruce started down the sidewalk, walking rapidly for half a block before he broke into a run. Even with the medication, the strain of running made his heart pound wildly. After only a few steps his legs felt wild and out of control. Sweat ran in rivulets down his back, soaking his T-shirt. But he wasn't going to stop running—not until he reached Lila's apartment. It wasn't far from the station, and he was desperate to see her.

When the complex came into view, Bruce allowed himself to slow his pace to a trot. He was dripping with sweat and gasping for breath as he limped up the brick walkway to Lila's unit. Lila would know what to do. Lila would help him.

"Lila!" Bruce called, pounding on her door. "Lila, please, I need you!" He pounded harder, then tried the knob. Her door was locked. Bruce stumbled back off her porch, still calling her name as he made his way around the building to her bedroom window. The curtains were drawn tight. He slammed his open hand against the glass in frustration.

Why isn't Lila around when I need her? he wondered. It seemed like he'd done nothing but look for her for the last three days. He could be *dying* for all Lila cared—he *was* dying.

What if I never see her again? An icy chill passed through him. *No. No, that's not going to happen!*

The little sidewalk lantern in front of Lila's apartment caught Bruce's pant leg as he lurched by. Cursing, he wheeled around and kicked it, his boot scattering glass in all directions. The sound had a strange, soothing effect on him. It seemed to release his frustration somehow, to calm his fear. Before he knew what he was doing, Bruce ran to the next lantern and kicked it too. It was satisfying watching the glass shards fly out across the closely clipped green lawn. He kicked the next, then the next until all six lanterns lay in ruins, the broken glass like a shattered patchwork against the lawn. *Beyond fixing*, he thought. *Just like my life*.

"Watch out, you lucky guys!" Jessica happily waggled her toes and admired her fresh pedicure. "Here comes Jessica Wakefield!"

She screwed the polish brush back onto the bottle as she swung her feet off the bed and down to the floor. The white toilet paper she'd wound between her toes contrasted sharply with the tan of her bare feet. Those strappy new sandals were going to look even better on her now.

The dedication of the Beringer Wing was less than an hour away, and all Jessica had left to do was pick out the perfect dress. Jessica heel-walked over to her closet, adjusting the white terry cloth bath towel she had wrapped around her body. But the sound of her dorm-room door flying open violently stopped her in her tracks.

"What did you do to me, Jessica?" Bruce Patman bellowed from the doorway. In two giant steps he dashed over to where she stood and grabbed her shoulders hard.

"Bruce! Let go!" she protested indignantly, grabbing at her towel to keep it from falling down. "How dare you barge in here without knocking!"

"Don't you talk to me that way," Bruce shot back, his voice low and menacing. "After what you did to me—"

135

"I have no idea what you're talking about," Jessica interrupted, backing away frantically. "But if you smear my toenail polish, I swear I'll kill you."

Bruce laughed—a crazy, ugly laugh. "A little late for that now, isn't it?" he asked, lowering his face to within inches of Jessica's. His pupils were wild and dilated, and an odor of sweat clung to him. Jessica shrank away. At first she'd only been embarrassed to be barged in on. Now Bruce was actually starting to scare her.

"Get out of my room," she ordered, pointing at the door. But Bruce didn't move a muscle. "Get out or I'll scream!"

"Scream away," he urged, gripping her shoulders harder. "Knock yourself out."

Jessica opened her mouth to scream, then changed her mind. She didn't really want half the girls on the hall rushing in and finding her half dressed with Bruce. Besides, it would be a sorry day in her life when she couldn't handle Bruce on her own.

"What's the matter with you, Bruce?" Jessica asked nervously.

"Why don't *you* tell *me?*"

"What—what do you mean?" Jessica squinted, trying hard to sort through his babbling.

"*You* did this to me, Jessica! Why?" Bruce yelled, shaking her hard, his voice growing

136

louder and more hysterical with every word. "That party . . . it wasn't *my* idea! But you messed up. I didn't curl up and die like I was supposed to, did I? No! No, you should have used *more*. What kind of poison was it?"

"*Poison!*" Jessica exclaimed. "You're delirious! I don't even know what you're talking about."

Bruce shook her so roughly that her head snapped back and forth. "I'm not kidding, Jessica—what's the antidote?"

"I don't know!"

"The antidote, Jessica!" Bruce screamed, forcing her back against the wall.

Jessica let out a strangled cry as her head hit the wall, her back and shoulders pinned tightly. Her heart hammered at her rib cage, and her breaths were short and harsh with fear. "Stop it!" she yelled, slapping him across the face with all her strength. "Let go of me right *now!*"

The blow raised an angry red patch on the sallow skin of his cheek. Then, very slowly, he released her shoulders and backed away, shaking his head as if confused.

"What's going on here, Bruce?" Jessica demanded, sensing she'd gained the upper hand.

Bruce's face was blank. "I—I'm sorry," he stuttered. Then he collapsed onto Elizabeth's bed and lay back on the pillow. Jessica stood her ground, staring down at him angrily. He looked even worse than he had that morning, and she wouldn't have thought that was possible.

"Are you still sick?" she asked.

"I'm dying."

Leave it to Bruce to turn a hangover into a terminal illness, Jessica thought. "Yeah, right. In that case, how about doing it somewhere else?"

Bruce grimaced and sat up on the bed. The motion seemed to pain him, and Jessica felt a little shock course through her. His face was so pale and drawn—yes, he *looked* like he was dying.

"Jeez, Bruce. Are you all right?" she asked, suddenly concerned.

"No, I'm not all right," Bruce croaked.

Jessica pulled her bathrobe off her desk chair and put it on over her towel before she sat down on her own bed, facing Bruce. "Tell me what happened."

"Someone is trying to kill me. I know, it sounds insane, but I passed out and woke up in the hospital. I've been poisoned. And if I don't find the antidote, I'm going to die. You have to help me, Jessica," he pleaded. "The police can't do anything, and Lila—I don't know where she is. You're the only one who knows exactly what I did last night. Help me retrace my steps."

Jessica heard his story with disbelief. Bruce poisoned? "What makes you think I'll help you?" she asked nastily. "I mean, after all, don't you think *I* did it?"

Bruce rubbed at his sweat-drenched forehead with one shaky hand. "I don't know what got into me before. I'm desperate, OK? I know you didn't do it."

"*How* do you know?"

"Because it doesn't make sense. I'm sure you would have enjoyed poisoning me far more in high school."

Jessica couldn't stifle a laugh, and Bruce joined her, collapsing into coughs. His face turned serious once again.

"I'm begging you, Jessica. You've got to help me. If you don't, I'm not going to make it."

"OK. I'll do it. But on one condition."

"What?"

"Change out of that sweaty old T-shirt. You totally reek."

"Do you think you could hurry up?" Bruce asked impatiently, herding Jessica toward the passenger side of his Porsche. "We've already wasted an hour." It was more like fifteen minutes, but it seemed like a *year* to Bruce.

"You don't look well enough to drive," Jessica protested.

"I got this far, didn't I?" he countered. "Get in."

With a huffy show of reluctance Jessica climbed in and buckled her seat belt. Bruce threw the car into gear, screeching out of the parking lot behind Dickenson Hall and onto the street.

If he didn't need her help so badly, he'd have left Jessica at home. First she'd had to get dressed, and then she'd gone searching for an old shirt of Steven's that she'd borrowed. Even though it was literally a matter of life and death, Jessica had insisted that she wouldn't go anywhere with him until he put on a clean shirt.

The tight cuffs of the long-sleeved chambray shirt annoyed him now as he steered the Porsche, and Bruce unbuttoned them as he drove and pushed the sleeves impatiently up his forearms. "We'll start at the Blue Lagoon," he announced, steering around a corner. "Maybe the bartender saw something."

Jessica nodded. "Whatever. But I still think that if someone poisoned you, it had to have been one of those sleazes at Jack Johnson's party."

"Those are my frat brothers," Bruce said impatiently. "Just because you don't like them doesn't mean they're sleazes."

"Puh-leeze! Jack Johnson is the biggest sleaze on the face of the earth," Jessica returned with conviction. "Any guy who would pinch a girl's butt ought to be locked up. And a guy who would help *another* guy pinch her butt is even lower."

Bruce was starting to wonder if she even grasped the situation. All she seemed concerned about were clean shirts, ruined toenail polish, and a few harmless losers at a frat party.

"Hey!" Jessica exclaimed. "Check it out!" She pointed out a flashy red convertible, top up, approaching them from the opposite direction.

Bruce groaned, but as the vintage MG passed them, he caught a flash of blond hair and a very familiar face. Impulsively he cranked the wheel around, sending the Porsche into a wide, skidding U-turn.

"Bruce!" Jessica screamed. "What are you doing?"

"I just saw something I want to follow up on," he replied grimly, fighting for control of the car. The Porsche stopped fishtailing, and Bruce regained speed immediately. "Thanks for the tip, Jessica. I might have missed him otherwise."

"Who?"

"The guy I was drinking with before you came in last night. He's in our film class."

"What's his name?"

"I don't know."

"Well, what does he look like?"

"He's just a guy, all right? Stop asking so many questions." Bruce applied more pressure to the accelerator to keep up with the MG, which had begun traveling faster.

Of the few things Bruce could recall from the night before, he vividly remembered Mr. Blond shooting his mouth off. That whole story about his girlfriend being found dead had stunk to high heaven. Maybe he'd even killed her himself. And if he'd killed before, what was to stop him from killing again?

But why would this total stranger want to poison me? Bruce wondered. *To keep me quiet about his girlfriend?* No, Bruce didn't really know anything about the woman's death, nothing concrete. And where would Mr. Blond have found the chance—or the idea?

Then, with a jolt, Bruce's blood ran cold. Mr. Blond had given Bruce one of his own beers the night before.

He'd also been in the film library the day Bruce had left behind his copy of *The Victim*.

Chapter Nine

"Hurry up!" Jessica urged, straining forward in the passenger seat. "He's getting away."

"I see that," Bruce snapped irritably. "He must know we're following him."

"We're going to lose him," Jessica warned.

"No, we're not." Bruce gave the Porsche more gas to be sure.

Moments later the SVU campus came into view, and Bruce had to slow down. There were pedestrians and bicyclists everywhere, and the streets had become much narrower. But thankfully the red MG convertible slowed down too.

Then it happened—a light up ahead turned red just as Mr. Blond ran through it. By the time Bruce got to the intersection, hordes of students were crossing the street, preventing him from following.

"Get out of my way!" he yelled out the

window, leaning on the car horn. A few startled students scattered, but most of them stopped in the crosswalk to stare at him. "Move it!" he hollered. By the time the crowd had cleared, the red MG was nowhere to be seen.

"We lost him," Jessica said.

"For now," Bruce admitted. "He can't have gone very far. This street dead-ends into the campus."

Bruce drove down the narrow street, his eyes scanning everywhere for the MG. There were no side streets the other driver could have turned off on, but there were parking lots everywhere, and he could easily have ducked into one to wait for Bruce to pass. Bruce was afraid that if he turned into a parking lot to look around, the other car would streak past on the road back into town and lose itself for good.

Bruce looked down at his hands. They gripped the steering wheel uncertainly, pale and shaky, and the veins stood out blue against his whitening flesh. He closed his eyes briefly, and silver flakes floated through the darkness behind his eyelids. The buzzing in his ears made it hard to hear, and every muscle in his body ached. Driving the car had taken more strength than he had. But he *had* to find Mr. Blond—he was the only lead Bruce had.

Bruce took a chance and turned into the film-school parking lot. "Keep an eye out for that

MG," he told Jessica as he cruised through the lot. If Mr. Blond was going to try to hide somewhere, it made sense he'd pick a familiar place.

"I see it. I see it!" Jessica squealed excitedly.

Bruce glanced across the rows in the direction Jessica was pointing. Sure enough, the MG was there, tucked into the last space on the row beneath a couple of trees—a place Bruce never could have spotted from the road. "Gotcha," he breathed, looking for a place to park himself. The lot was surprisingly jammed for so late in the afternoon, however, and Bruce had to do two full, agonizing circuits before he finally found a space where someone else was pulling out.

"We'll split up," Bruce announced, hustling Jessica out of the car and across the parking lot toward the film-school buildings. "We can cover more ground that way."

"I don't even know what this guy looks like," Jessica protested, struggling to keep up with him in the short red dress and strappy sandals she'd insisted on wearing. "And what do you expect me to do if I find him? I won't know where you are."

As much as Bruce wanted to argue, he couldn't deny she had a point. "Fine," he growled. "We'll stay together." They'd reached the edge of the pavement, where a large crowd of students, faculty, and parents milled about in the courtyard outside the entrance to the new wing. Many more people were streaming inside through the open doors.

"Oh no!" he exclaimed. "Look at this crowd! It's that stupid dedication ceremony for the Beringer Wing."

"*Some* of us wanted to go to it," Jessica whined.

"Excuse *me*," he returned bitterly. "But something more important came up. Come on. Let's go in."

Jessica looked confused but hopeful. "You want to go to the dedication now? I thought we were—"

"No, I *don't* want to go to the *dedication!*" Bruce interrupted, struggling to keep calm. "I just have a feeling that guy is in there."

Jessica's expression fell, and Bruce grabbed her by the wrist as they entered the crowded courtyard, passed through the open doors, and walked into the new Beringer Wing. The building was beautifully designed, with a high-ceilinged entry area and curving staircases to the second level on either side, but Bruce barely noticed his surroundings as he dragged Jessica through the crowd. "Look for tall, handsome guys with blond hair," he instructed her.

"Mmm." Jessica brightened again. "No problem."

They pushed their way through several large exhibition rooms, the crush of people becoming denser in each one, and ultimately into an enormous auditorium, which was packed to standing room only. Bruce and Jessica stood in the back, Bruce straining up on his toes to scan the crowd for Mr. Blond.

Just then the lights in the auditorium dimmed and a spotlight picked up the lectern placed on the stage at the front of the room. Professor Gordon somberly strode out to the podium.

"It is my honor," he proclaimed as the crowd noise dropped to a hush, "to open these dedication ceremonies for the new Beringer Wing of the Sweet Valley University Film School. Belinda Beringer was a beautiful and gifted young woman, and even as we celebrate this outstanding addition to our university, we must do so with a certain sadness. Those of us who knew Belinda will never forget her—her enthusiasm, her kindness, and the tragedy of her early death." The professor's voice quavered slightly at the mention of Belinda's suicide, and the audience nodded in silent understanding.

"But today we wish to celebrate Belinda's life," Professor Gordon continued bravely, "not dwell on her death. And to begin that celebration, I have the honor now of unveiling her portrait." Professor Gordon gestured dramatically to the wall behind him, and a black velvet drape dropped to the floor, revealing a large oil painting of an attractive young woman with long, dark

147

and intense hazel eyes. The audience cheered and applauded, but Bruce turned his attention back to the crowd, searching, as Professor Gordon announced the next speaker.

"Oh, wow," Jessica whispered at his side. "Now *there's* a tall blond babe. I practically drool every time he walks into class."

"Where?" Bruce whispered urgently.

Jessica pointed to the stage. "Right up there."

Bruce looked up at the podium and froze in amazement. Professor Gordon was walking off the stage, and taking his place at the podium was Mr. Blond!

"Thank you," he said, adjusting the microphone to suit his considerable height while the applause died down. "Belinda Beringer was my fiancée."

The audience reacted with expressions of muted sympathy, but Bruce heard the news in shock. Belinda Beringer was mixed up with that loser? What would a class act like Belinda want with *him*? It certainly wasn't his money. No matter how rich he claimed to be, the Beringers could bury him in cash.

"I . . . I'm still not over Belinda's death," Mr. Blond continued, a catch in his voice. "Sometimes I think I'll never get over it. But being here today—seeing all the people who loved her and miss her—really helps."

Of course! Bruce thought. *Belinda Beringer*

was the woman he had been talking about at the bar—the one he'd practically admitted to killing! It was all starting to come together. The guy had murdered his own fiancée! And if he'd killed Belinda, what was to stop him from killing Bruce too?

Bruce shook with excitement from the discovery, but he still had no idea *why* Mr. Blond would want him dead. There was no good reason.

"What's this guy's name?" Bruce whispered to Jessica. "I missed it before."

"Marcus. Marcus Stanton," she replied, mesmerized, not taking her eyes off the stage.

"Marcus," Bruce repeated softly, the name triggering an alarm in his mind. "Oh no."

"What?" Jessica asked.

"Nothing," Bruce muttered. "Let me think."

"Rich and beautiful . . ." Marcus's words from the night before echoed in Bruce's mind. *"She dumped me . . . this boyfriend of hers is a major jerk . . . we would have been so perfect together. . . ."*

Lila hadn't just cheated on him—she'd cheated on him with a murderer. A murderer who was obsessed with rich, beautiful women.

And Bruce was the only person in his way.

"I remember when Belinda wrote her first screenplay," Marcus reminisced, his strong hands gripping the front edge of the podium.

Jessica leaned forward, hanging on every word. Not only was Marcus Stanton's tribute to his lost love incredibly moving and romantic, but he looked extremely tasty while he delivered it.

"What I remember most was her excitement—she was absolutely on fire. Whenever she got excited like that, her eyes used to light up like gold. I think it was her passion that drew people to—"

"Come on," Bruce whispered loudly, grabbing Jessica by the upper arm. "We're leaving."

"Not now," Jessica complained. "I'm listening to this."

Bruce clenched his fists in apparent frustration. "That's the guy who poisoned me! Come on—we'll catch him backstage. You can listen to him some more when I get him to confess."

"You can't be serious—" Jessica began, but without another word Bruce jerked her nearly off her feet in the direction of the rear exit. As he pulled her through the crowd, his fingers digging into the flesh of her upper arm, Jessica noticed that his skin had a slight bluish cast and his grip wasn't as strong as it had been in her room earlier. He stumbled when he walked and rubbed continually at his eyes, as if trying to clear his vision. Even so, the expression on his face was so determined, so intense, that it suddenly gave her goose bumps.

"You're really dying, aren't you?" she whispered as Bruce dragged her mercilessly down the hallway outside the auditorium. "I mean, this is for real, isn't it?"

"Yes," was all Bruce said. He let her arm go, and side by side they ran down the hall toward the backstage entrance.

Thank goodness she's finally come around, Bruce thought as he and Jessica reached the end of the hall. *And not a moment too soon.* With sweaty hands Bruce tried the knob on the backstage door, but it was locked.

"You wait here, and if he comes out, scream," Bruce ordered. "I'm going to look for another way in."

Jessica nodded, her blue-green eyes wide and worried, and for once she didn't argue.

Charged with adrenaline, Bruce ran another fifty feet to the very end of the hall and found a second door. This one was locked too. Frustrated, Bruce rattled the knob, kicking the door for emphasis. He was heading back toward Jessica when the door opened unexpectedly.

"Can I help you?" inquired a matronly looking woman.

"Uh, yes, actually," Bruce replied, hurrying back to the doorway. "I . . . uh . . . I was supposed to meet my friend Marcus backstage before his speech, but I got held up in traffic."

The woman didn't say anything, didn't move; she only raised her eyebrows a bit.

Bruce thought fast. "Talking about Belinda is so hard for Marcus. I really appreciate your letting me in like this so I can be there for him when he's done," Bruce pressed, slipping one foot inside the door. "Thank you *so* much."

"You're welcome," the woman said, shrugging and walking away.

Bruce braced his foot against the open door and waved Jessica over. "Come on," Bruce hissed. "Hurry up!"

Jessica raced down the hallway, and together they walked inside. As far as Bruce could tell, they were somewhere under the stage. It was dark and low ceilinged, with wooden support struts jutting at all angles.

"Losing Belinda is a burden I'll carry for as long as I live," Marcus's deep, amplified voice intoned from up above them. "And yet I know that she would want me—would want us all—to move forward and live a happy life. That's what I'll try to do, in her memory."

What a sick piece of work! Bruce thought angrily as the end of Marcus's speech was greeted by tumultuous applause. *Of course he wants to move forward and live a happy life—with my girlfriend!*

"Shhh!" Bruce hissed, irritated. "He'll be coming offstage any second now."

152

Jessica nodded and pointed at the wall on their right, where a man's shadow loomed. Bruce cringed when he saw Marcus Stanton appear, running down a short staircase just a few yards away. Both he and Jessica backed farther into the shadows. At the bottom of the stairs Marcus glanced around for a moment, then wandered away. Without a word Jessica and Bruce crept after him.

Marcus moved slowly down a hall and through an open door. Holding his breath, Bruce sidled down the same hall and peeked through the doorway into a small sitting room. Marcus was alone.

Bruce charged into the tiny room, Jessica right behind him. "Shut the door, Jessica," Bruce ordered in a low voice. Jessica quickly closed the door, and Bruce moved toward Marcus menacingly.

"Hey! What are you doing here?" Marcus asked, his voice quavering with anxiety. "What the hell is wrong with you?"

"That's what *I'd* like to know. And after our little conversation at the bar last night, I've got a hunch that you can tell me."

"I don't know what you're talking about," Marcus said, his eyes shifting toward the door. He looked trapped, desperate. Suddenly he sprang toward the exit, but Bruce cut him off halfway, shoving him into the wall. Marcus slammed up against the plaster with a terrific crash, and Bruce pinned his shoulders to the wall. Marcus's deep brown eyes searched Bruce's frantically for a moment, looking away when a sudden sweat erupted on his brow under his crop of blond hair. He shook in Bruce's grip and strained toward the doorway.

"I know what you did to Belinda," Bruce said slowly, letting every word dig deep and sink in. "You're not going to get away with it—with *any* of it."

The fierce and unexpected blow that Marcus loosed to his stomach bent Bruce over double. Marcus slipped away as Bruce reeled backward in excruciating pain, his arms crossed over his gut.

"Stop him, Jessica!" Bruce wheezed, but Jessica stood rooted in place as Marcus yanked open the door and sprinted down the hall. "Go after him!" Bruce pleaded. "See where he goes!"

Instead Jessica ran to his side. "Are you all right?" she asked, trying to help him stand upright. "Did he hurt you?"

"Do I look all right?" Bruce countered, gasping for the air to speak. "Come on. He'll probably run for his car. We have to catch him."

Every step was agony for Bruce as he and Jessica hurried out to the parking lot. If he'd been in pain before, being punched in the stomach had taken things to a whole new level. Patches of blackness passed before his eyes, and he thought he would retch at any second. He couldn't catch his breath, and his legs could barely support him. He *felt* like he would die at any second.

"There he goes!" Jessica shouted suddenly, pointing at the red MG. It streaked through the parking lot exit and onto the street, headed toward town.

"You'll have to drive," Bruce said, tossing Jessica the Porsche keys. "I don't think I can right now."

Jessica looked far more shocked than she had when he'd told her he'd been poisoned. She held the car keys out in front of her as if they had been timed to explode. "You're kidding, right?"

In answer Bruce opened the right-side door and collapsed into the passenger seat. "Let's go."

Jessica hesitated only a second, then leaped into the driver's seat. A second later the car was in gear and she was laying rubber all the way across the parking lot. "Whooo!" she hooted happily, careening around the corner and onto the street. "This thing *hauls!*"

Bruce closed his eyes and tried not to think about his engine, his suspension, his performance tires. The stakes were too big now—his life was literally in Jessica's hands. Still, she didn't have to drive like a *total* maniac. He wished he could grab the wheel away from her and steer from the passenger side.

Not that he possibly could have. The pain in

his stomach had receded slightly, but the other pains were getting worse. Bruce looked down at his powerless hands. They shook noticeably, and the skin seemed almost translucent—translucent and blurry. With a gasp he looked through the windshield to see that the cars ahead of them were fuzzy, coming into focus only intermittently. He squinted and prayed that he wasn't losing his vision.

"There he is!" Jessica announced excitedly. "We've got him, Bruce!"

With an effort Bruce made out the speeding red convertible up ahead.

"He's getting on the freeway," Jessica reported, steering up the on-ramp smoothly. To Bruce's dismay, he saw a bright blur of what seemed like hundreds of headlights around them; traffic on the freeway was heavy. Soon the Porsche was snarled up behind two big trucks in the middle of the after-work commute. "Rush hour," Jessica said sadly as the red car appeared to creep farther away from them in the orange haze of the setting sun. "What a drag."

"We have to catch him," Bruce urged, the rapidly darkening sky reminding him how little time he had left. "*Do* something, Jessica!"

Jessica reacted by honking the car horn in loud blasts. The commuters in the cars around them slowed to stare, leaving her a little room to maneuver. Darting and weaving through the stop-and-go traffic, Jessica guided the Porsche over to the paved, right-hand emergency shoulder. "Hang on," she advised grimly as she reached the open space. Then she stomped on the accelerator.

The car leaped forward, and Bruce gripped the edges of his seat as Jessica fought the steering wheel to keep the Porsche from drifting into the concrete wall to their right. A chorus of protesting car horns erupted from the vehicles in the slow lane on the left as the little black sports car rocketed by an inch from their passenger sides.

"Watch out!" Bruce shouted as a minivan just ahead of them began easing onto the shoulder. Jessica leaned on the horn and shot through the narrowing gap between the minivan and the wall without reducing her speed in the slightest.

"Yeah! Did you see that?" she hollered triumphantly.

"Keep driving like that and we'll *both* end up dead," Bruce grumbled, not wanting to admit to Jessica how grateful he was to her for risking her own life to help him. She probably wouldn't have noticed anyway; she seemed to be having too much fun. They were gaining fast now, and if Marcus remained stuck in the stopped traffic up ahead . . .

"Oh *no!*" Bruce shouted as Marcus's car found a little open space and darted suddenly to the right. "He's getting off the freeway!"

"I'm right behind him," Jessica said, her eyes glued to the road ahead. She followed him down the off-ramp practically on his bumper.

The convertible flew down a couple of major city streets, then careened up a narrow side road in the direction of the nearby foothills. "Oh, jeez," Jessica groaned, glancing at Bruce. "I think he's heading for Crestview."

Bruce echoed Jessica's groan. Crestview was a mess of hairpin turns etched into steep hillsides and skirting narrow, brush-filled canyons. Cars made fatal mistakes on those roads every day, even in broad daylight. And daylight was far behind them now. It would be pitch dark by the time they reached Crestview, where the widely spaced, luxurious houses were all set far back from the road and streetlights were unheard of.

The last traces of light had faded when Jessica made the first hairpin turn up the mountainside, tires squealing. The Porsche's headlights made a wild arc across the brush-covered terrain in front of them, then found the road again. "I don't like this," Jessica muttered under her breath, her hands clenching the wheel.

"You're doing fine," Bruce encouraged her, wishing he were the one behind the wheel. He forced himself to look away from the treacherous canyons that extended to the edge of the narrow, winding road and focus instead on the taillights of the car in front of them. Marcus seemed to know the road like the back of his hand—he took the turns at top speed, sometimes on only two wheels. But the Porsche was a more maneuverable and powerful car than an MG, and Jessica was driving it like a professional.

"Stay on him, Jess," Bruce urged excitedly. "Don't give him any room."

Jessica cranked the wheel through another heart-stopping turn, narrowing the distance between the two cars. They were so close now that the Porsche's headlights reflected off the convertible's bumper, rendering them practically useless for illuminating the road.

Without warning Marcus whipped his car into an impossibly sharp right turn. The Porsche's headlights beamed out into the open night, revealing what was in front of them: a guardrail, with only the dark sky behind it.

"Bruce!" Jessica screamed, trying to make the turn. But it was too late. As Marcus's car sped off noisily up the hillside the Porsche crashed through the flimsy metal guardrail and sailed out into space, nothing underneath it but the blackness of the night.

Chapter
Ten

"Well, that was delicious, as always," Mrs. Fowler said, putting down her fork. "I couldn't eat another bite."

Lila smiled, glad that her mother had enjoyed her dinner. "But you still have to have some dessert, Mom. After all, it *is* your birthday."

"I'll tell you what," Mrs. Fowler said. "I'll put some sweetener in my coffee and we'll call it dessert."

"Dad!" Lila protested. Lila had commissioned Andre's famous pastry chef to make a special birthday cake. Her surprise would be spoiled if her mother insisted on skipping dessert.

Mr. Fowler came quickly to Lila's aid. "What do you say we take a couple of turns around the dance floor before we make any irreversible decisions about dessert?" he asked his wife.

"Good idea!" Lila put in. "I'll have the waiter clear the dishes and bring the coffee while you're gone."

"That sounds wonderful," Mrs. Fowler agreed. With a playful flourish Mr. Fowler squired her off to the formal, polished oak dance floor.

As soon as Lila's parents were gone the waiter came to take the plates away and freshen the table. He brushed the crumbs off the wine-colored table-cloth, replaced the white linen napkins with clean ones, and fussed with the candles, flowers, and crystal water glasses until everything was as beautiful as before the Fowlers first sat down.

"Shall I bring the coffee now?" he asked Lila. "Or would you prefer to wait?"

"No, please bring it," she instructed him. "And bring the cake out too, so that everything's ready when my parents get back."

"Very good, Ms. Fowler." The waiter nodded and strode off across the dining room. Lila was alone at the table.

Lila was glad that Andre's was her mother's favorite restaurant because she loved it too. Everything about it was classy, from the crystal chandeliers to the expensive china and silver on the tables to the impeccable service. Eating at Andre's always made Lila feel like a queen. She glanced across the restaurant toward the dance floor, where her parents were waltzing with some other couples to the music provided by a live string ensemble.

"Lila!" exclaimed a woman to her left. "Lila Fowler, is that you?"

Lila turned and drew her breath in with surprise. "Shelly Mitchell! I don't believe it. What a coincidence! I was just talking about you the other day."

"All good, I hope," Shelly remarked with a warm smile. In the years since Lila had seen her old friend from camp, Shelly had clearly matured. Her simple black dress was elegant and tasteful, and her wildly curly brown hair was tamed into a sophisticated twist. Shelly's escort was a tall, red-haired man who Lila had never seen before.

"This is Mike Jessup," Shelly said, introducing him. "Mike, this is an old friend from camp, Lila Fowler."

"Pleased to meet you," he said politely.

"Likewise," said Lila. "Sit down for a minute, won't you? This is so weird! It must be Shelly Mitchell week."

"What do you mean?" Shelly asked as she and Mike took seats at the table.

"Well, I haven't seen you in *ages*. Then just a couple of days ago I met a friend of yours from Hillhaven—and now here you are!"

"Really?" she asked. "I do miss Hillhaven. Who was it?"

"Marcus Stanton. From the tennis team."

"Marcus Stanton?" Shelly repeated, her forehead wrinkling with confusion. "I don't know a Marcus Stanton."

"Oh, but you must," Lila insisted. "Tall,

blond, and way too gorgeous? He recognized *your* name immediately."

Shelly shook her head. "He's mistaken. I don't know him. Anyway, I'm positive there was no Marcus Stanton on the tennis team. Are you sure he went to Hillhaven?"

"That's what he said," Lila replied. "I guess I've got it mixed up somehow."

But Lila knew she wasn't mixed up. As Shelly and Mike said their good-byes and moved on to their own table, she couldn't suppress a slight chill.

There was *definitely* something wrong about Marcus Stanton. Lila had sensed it the night before, when he'd gotten so angry after the movie, but she'd explained it away as a simple injury to his pride. But now that Shelly denied even knowing him, the feeling was back, stronger than ever. The guy was not only strange, but he was a liar too. Why on earth would Marcus lie about something as trivial as attending Hillhaven? Whose Hillhaven shirt had he been wearing when she met him? What else had he lied about?

Just thinking about Marcus's handsome, seemingly wholesome face and blinding smile gave Lila the creeps. She'd been *right* to give him the brush-off. In fact, it would suit Lila just fine if she never saw the guy again.

The car seemed to hang in the air forever. Jessica's scream cut through the night, but it seemed to reach Bruce's ears in slow motion. For a moment he almost convinced himself that none of this was happening. They weren't hurtling off the hillside into nothingness, they weren't plummeting toward the earth. They weren't about to crash and die.

Is it possible to kill a guy twice? Bruce wondered in a flash as the Porsche nosed down toward the canyon, the ground rushing up to meet them in the twin beams of the headlights.

"Bruce!" Jessica screamed again. "Nooo!"

Then impact.

The car slammed into earth with more noise than Bruce would have imagined possible. Jessica was screaming, the Porsche groaned and shrieked, and the brush in front of them and on either side scratched and snapped as the sports car slid headlong down the steep canyon. Then, miraculously, they stopped. Bruce held himself motionless, unable to believe he was still alive, let alone right-side up and unharmed. Maybe he wasn't alive. Maybe this was death.

But the sound of Jessica crying softly and the sight of her hands still gripping the now useless wheel convinced him that he—both of them—had survived.

"Are you OK?" he asked, his voice shaking.

Jessica nodded. "You?"

Bruce shrugged. "Everything's relative." He stared forward into the light of a single headlight, which had been knocked askew. It leered up crazily into the night, illuminating nothing but dust and empty darkness. The windshield was half covered with dirt and brush.

"I can't see anything," Bruce said, unfastening his seat belt. "There's a flashlight in the trunk. I'm going to get it." He opened the door, only to feel the car slip downhill a few more feet before it snagged on something and stopped.

"Eeek!" Jessica cried, her face ashen. "Don't you *dare* do that again, Bruce Patman!"

"Great," he muttered. "We survived the crash, and now the car wants to kill us." Until they were both safely out of the Porsche and standing on firm ground, there was no telling what their fate would be. Moving slowly, Bruce pushed his door open a little wider—the Porsche teetered precariously. He held his breath, afraid that even the smallest motion would send them hurtling down into the darkness again.

"Open your door," he whispered to Jessica. "*Very* slowly."

Jessica's hand barely moved, inching toward the handle as if it were a snake. The driver's door opened a sliver without incident.

"What if the car starts moving again?" Jessica asked in a tiny whisper.

"Then we'll just have to jump out of it. Now go on. But be *careful!*"

Jessica slowly pushed the door out a little farther,

then farther still. Finally it stood all the way open, and still the Porsche hadn't moved. Even so, the car seemed to be teetering on something. Barely balanced, right on the edge of . . . what?

"OK," said Bruce. "Take off your seat belt and get out."

Jessica glared at him, her eyes unfocused with fear, but she nodded slightly. Moving carefully, Jessica edged over in her seat as far as she could without actually getting out. The Porsche rocked a little.

"Go!" Bruce told her. "Jump!"

Jessica leaned forward out of the car and lunged into the darkness. Bruce heard her land in a crash of brush, then the car started sliding forward down the canyon again, rapidly gaining speed.

"Bruce!" He barely heard Jessica's thin, panicked cry from behind him. "Bruce, jump!"

Jump? It had been easier to say. But to actually do it . . .

"Juuump!" Jessica screamed frantically.

Bruce jumped. For a moment there was nothing underneath him, then he crashed into a large, dry bush that stabbed at his hands and scratched his face. He gripped it in the darkness, holding on as his feet scrabbled for footing on the steep hillside. His boots dug into the earth, and his hands relaxed slightly. He was out. He was alive.

It was then that Bruce heard the tremendous crash far below him. Turning, he squinted into the darkness, slowly realizing he was on the very edge of a steep slope—beyond him the canyon walls became nearly vertical. And somewhere, down in the darkness at the canyon bottom, was a heap of twisted metal that had once been his most cherished possession.

My Porsche! Bruce panicked. *It's ruined!* But then, to his total amazement, his next thought was, *Who cares?* That car had been his signature, his freedom, and even his best friend. But what was a Porsche, when you thought about it, compared to even a few more hours of life?

"Bruce! Oh, Bruce, thank goodness you're OK," he heard Jessica sob as her footsteps rustled toward him. "I thought—I thought you hadn't—"

"Stay where you are, Jessica," he yelled. "Don't move!"

He heard her drop to the ground, sobbing, and a strange feeling came over him. He had never in his wildest dreams imagined that he and Jessica Wakefield would share a moment like this, that she would cry hysterically at the possibility of his death. Of course, she had just come a hair's breadth away from being killed too. And Bruce was still a long way from being out of the woods.

"Come on," he said, pulling himself to his feet and heading in the direction of Jessica's sobs. "We have to find Marcus Stanton." He could barely make out the ground beneath him as he stumbled through the darkness, but eventually he saw a shape that moved as he came nearer—Jessica. "Come on," he repeated, offering her a hand. "Get up."

Wordlessly Jessica took the hand Bruce offered, but as he tried to pull her to her feet, he realized that he couldn't—he no longer had the strength. "Sorry," he murmured, shaken by his own weakness.

Jessica got up on her own. Her sobs slowed, then stopped as she faced Bruce on the path. "How are we going to get out of here?" she asked, her voice a scratchy whisper. "We can't even see."

"Yes, we can," Bruce insisted, determined to climb out of the canyon. "Just try to let your eyes adjust to the darkness." He strode forward, his own eyes trained on the slightly lighter path of raw earth the Porsche had churned up as it slid down the brushy hillside. He could hear Jessica picking her way along behind him in her sandals. After about fifteen minutes Bruce found that his eyes really *had* adjusted. He saw a much steeper section of canyon wall looming in front of him and, above that, the edge of the road.

"The road's just ahead. We're almost there," Bruce said hopefully, but suddenly he wondered why he was the one giving encouragement. The crash had produced a rush of adrenaline that had temporarily masked his illness, but now it was gone, used up. His strength was failing by the minute, and he could feel it ebbing away in waves timed with the quickness of his heartbeat. Bruce looked up at the nearly vertical, twenty-foot-high wall in front of him and knew he'd never be able to climb it. Dawn would find him still at the base of that cliff.

A cold rush of panic rose up in his throat, nearly choking him. He was going to die in a Crestview canyon.

"Bruce?" Jessica said tentatively, eyeing the dark wall before her. "I don't think I can climb that."

"Neither can I," Bruce admitted in a strangled, defeated voice. Then she heard him sink down onto the ground. Jessica hesitated a moment, then sat beside him.

"I'm sorry we didn't catch Marcus. I really tried," she offered.

"I know you did. You did all anyone could have." Bruce chuckled softly. "You were great, actually."

"Thanks." A silence fell between them. Jessica sat motionless, inhaling the strong scent of broken sage and scrub and going over the last few hours in her mind.

"Bruce?" she ventured again after a few minutes. "I'm sorry about the Porsche too." She winced, anticipating Bruce's reaction.

To her surprise, his lips curled into a slight, sad smile. "Don't worry, Jessica. I don't even care anymore."

"Well," she said. "I wanted you to know." Silence washed over them once again. There was nothing left to say.

Then a faint sound hummed through the night, growing louder as Jessica listened. A car was coming! But how could they flag it down? They had nothing—not even a flashlight. It would pass them. It would drive on through the night, and the driver would never know they were there unless they—she—did something.

Bruce's eyes widened in the darkness as if he was urging her to think of something. But as the engine noise grew louder, neither one of them moved. Bruce closed his eyes in apparent resignation, and Jessica did the same. How could she scale that wall in a matter of a few seconds? It was impossible. Soon their chance would be gone.

Suddenly she heard the screeching of brakes. "Check out that guardrail," a voice above them resounded. "Someone went over the edge—"

"Help!" Jessica screamed. "Help us! Please!"

Two car doors opened, then slammed quickly. "She's alive!" a different voice shouted.

"Help!" Jessica screamed again. "We can't get out!"

"Are you all right?" the first voice called down over the edge. "How many of you are there?"

"Just two," Bruce answered weakly. "We're OK. Please—can you get us out of here? Do you guys have a rope or something?"

"Even better," the second voice boomed. "We've got a winch."

"Oh, thank goodness!" Jessica cried, hardly believing their luck. With a motorized winch the men could easily pull them up the canyon wall—they wouldn't even have to climb.

"Lower it down," Bruce directed.

"Please!" Jessica added.

A minute later a cable snaked down the hillside, rustling the bushes. Jessica ran to it, then waited as Bruce caught up and tested his weight against it. The cable seemed strong and secure.

"Come on, Jessica," Bruce said, motioning to the makeshift loop at the end of the cable. "You're first."

Jessica put one foot in the loop the way Bruce showed her, then held on with both hands. "Use your free foot to push off the wall as you go up," Bruce advised. "Are you ready?"

"Ready," Jessica agreed nervously. Even though she was relieved that they'd be getting out of the canyon, knowing that she'd be dangling over a severe cliff on the end of a thin metal cable made her feel slightly terrified.

Bruce yelled for the men at the top to winch her up, and Jessica began a jerky, uncomfortable ascent. "Yeow!" she complained as she crashed into a large bush, but the winch drew her steadily upward, and soon she was halfway to the road. "You'd better not be looking up my dress, Bruce Patman," she warned before painfully bouncing off the canyon wall. "Ouch!"

With immense relief Jessica reached the top at last, and strong hands reached out for her. Seconds later she was standing on the pavement with two strange men, staring into the powerful headlights of a large white tow truck.

"Th-Thank you," she stammered, overcome with relief.

"Our pleasure," one of the men, a tall, stocky blond, assured her with a shy smile. The other man relowered the cable for Bruce. Bruce made the ascent relatively quickly, rappelling off the slope to miss the worst of the brush.

"You two are lucky we happened along," the winch operator said once Bruce was safely on the road.

"We sure are," Bruce agreed gratefully. "You saved my life. . . ." He trailed off, reminding Jessica of what lay ahead.

The man brushed off Bruce's thanks with an embarrassed gesture. "Shoot. We saved you a night out in the cold, maybe. Someone would have found you in the morning."

"Where's your car?" the blond asked, shining a powerful spotlight down into the canyon. "You want us to try to pull it out when it gets light?"

A hard, humorless laugh escaped Bruce's lips. "You can try—and keep whatever you recover. My car is history."

"That's usually the case when cars go off this turn," the blond remarked. "That and whoever's driving."

Jessica shivered, and not just from the cold.

"Would you guys be able to take us down the hill to a pay phone?" Bruce asked. "I'll pay you."

The guys shrugged off the offer. "We don't expect to be paid for helping people," the other guy said, opening the driver's door and boosting Jessica in. The cold, cracked vinyl of the seat stuck to her bare thighs, but Jessica hardly noticed. Soon all four of them were crammed in the tow truck's front cab and heading back down the hillside.

Jessica's mind churned as the truck worked its way through the turns. Bruce was sagging in his seat. A muscle in his cheek twitched convulsively, erratically. He needed to be in the hospital, not chasing some crazed killer all over Crestview. She had to get him to agree to rest and let the police chase Marcus.

If only Dr. Martin would discover the antidote! she thought. Then they could deal with Marcus later. "Have you checked that beeper Dr. Martin gave you?" Jessica asked Bruce suddenly, breaking the silence. "Maybe she's trying to get in touch with you."

Bruce reached down to his waistband. A horrified expression gripped his features.

"Oh no," he groaned. "It's gone."

Driving back to her apartment after dinner, Lila couldn't sort out the mess in her mind. Mrs.

Fowler's birthday had been near perfect—but that weird encounter with Shelly Mitchell was still making Lila's head spin.

Why had Marcus made up that story about going to Hillhaven and knowing Shelly? Was it to gain her trust so that she'd go out with him? Was he some kind of compulsive liar? Lila shuddered in spite of the fact that she'd turned on her car heater. She wished she'd never told Marcus where she lived.

Then she remembered something. She never *had* told him where she lived. How could he have known where to send her flowers after they'd first met? Could he have followed her to her apartment at some point without her realizing it? The thought made her skin crawl. And she'd actually invited him in before they'd gone out to the movies! What if he'd attacked her or something?

Lila pulled her car into the reserved space behind her building and cut the engine. The night seemed strangely dark as she sat in the sports car, lost in thought. She'd been a fool to get involved with a total stranger, especially when she already had a boyfriend, and now she was paying the price. The first chance she got, she'd tell Bruce everything. Bruce would forgive her. If necessary, Bruce would protect her.

Suddenly Lila was overcome with longing to see him. She could practically *feel* his arms around her, his reassuring kisses brushing her face. How pointless all their fighting had been!

It was time to make up. Lila flicked on the dome light above her head and glanced at her watch. It was late, but not too late to call him and ask him to come over.

Lila got out of the car, locked the door behind her, and headed toward her apartment. When she rounded the Dumpster and stepped out into the courtyard, however, she stopped in surprise. The courtyard was pitch black.

"What happened to the lights?" she wondered aloud, peering into the darkness for a glimpse of the sidewalk lanterns. She had never realized before how much safer those little garden lights made the courtyard feel.

After a moment's nervous hesitation Lila started forward through the darkness, wild thoughts racing through her brain. What if Marcus were lurking somewhere, waiting for her to come home? Maybe he'd even turned off the lights somehow! With every tentative step she took down the path to her apartment, she became more afraid.

Suddenly there was a loud crashing in the bushes to her right. "Aaaaugh!" she screamed reflexively as a low-slung white missile streaked past her legs. It was only the neighbor's cat.

"Phew!" she breathed in relief, her stomach up in her throat. Her heart was pounding so hard, she felt dizzy.

Finally she reached her porch. Keys gripped

tightly in her shaking hand, Lila fumbled with the doorknob in the darkness. The lock turned, the door swung open, and Lila sighed with relief. She was just reaching for the light switch inside the door when she heard familiar-sounding booted footsteps behind her.

Bruce! she thought happily. He'd finally come. Turning back to face the courtyard, Lila waited, but the footsteps stopped on the path a few feet away. She could only dimly make out the shape of a tall man standing on the brickwork.

"Bruce?" she said uneasily, suddenly nervous again.

In a single, unexpected motion the dark form leaped onto the porch, lunging for her. Terrified, Lila wheeled around frantically, trying to get inside her open door, but her attacker was too quick for her. His arms closed around her waist and he pushed her into the dark apartment, kicking the door shut behind them.

Lila screamed, but too late. A gloved hand covered her mouth instantly, cutting off the sound almost before it started. Her assailant's other arm squeezed her tight, making it almost impossible to breathe.

Stop it! Let me go! she wanted to scream, but the glove over her mouth pressed down harder, keeping her silent. She struggled wildly, desperate to break free, but now her attacker was pushing her in the direction of the bedroom. Lila was so overcome with dread as the man forced her through her bedroom door that it almost paralyzed her. She stopped struggling for a second, fear making her weak. Then, with all the strength she possessed, she brought one of her ultra-high heels down hard on her attacker's foot.

Her attacker roared in pain—his deep cry twisted into an inhuman, animal sound. Lila sprang away and ran for the bedroom door, but the man blocked her exit. Instinctively she ran toward the bathroom. If she locked herself in, she could scream for help out the tiny window. She had barely reached the bathroom doorway when her attacker grabbed her again, tackling her hard from behind.

Lila fell forward into the bathroom, her arms stretched blindly in front of her. A shock of pain exploded in her head, and bright reds and blues shimmered behind her closed eyes. She had hit her head on something cold and hard—the toilet, the tub, she wasn't sure. A hollow thunk reverberated through her skull before her body went limp and slid the rest of the way down to the hard tile floor. The coolness of tile against one slack cheek and the sense of relief as her attacker climbed off her were the last things Lila felt. She was drifting. She was floating.

A man's voice spoke to her from far away. Lila heard the words, but they made no sense. Then everything went black.

Chapter
Eleven

"I know you're not going to like this," Jessica told Bruce as the tow truck disappeared from sight. "But I think you ought to rest. We should go back to the hospital."

"No way," Bruce said grimly, digging through his pockets for change.

Their rescuers had dropped them off at a gas station at the bottom of the hill, and now Bruce stood in front of a pay phone, Jessica beside him. They both looked horrible—scratched and filthy—but that was the last thing on Bruce's mind as he dropped a quarter into the slot and dialed information.

"What city, please?" inquired the information operator.

"Crestview," Bruce responded, praying he was right. "A number for Marcus Stanton, please."

"I have no listing for that party," said the operator.

"Try Sweet Valley," Bruce directed before she could hang up.

"I'm sorry, sir. No listing."

"Look, I don't know where he lives," Bruce admitted desperately. "Try southern California."

"I have no listing for a Marcus Stanton at all," said the operator. "Thank you for calling." The line went dead.

Bruce slammed the receiver back into the cradle angrily. "Now what?" he demanded, more for his own benefit than Jessica's. It was getting late. Very late. Bruce glared at his traitorous watch as if *it* were the enemy. Quarter to ten. Late, but not too late.

"Maybe you could get his number through the registrar's office," Jessica suggested.

Bruce thought about it only a second. "Not at this time of night." No, he'd have to track Marcus some other way. But how? Suddenly Bruce remembered—Lila! Maybe she knew where he lived.

"Who are you calling now?" Jessica asked as Bruce dropped another quarter into the phone.

"Lila."

"Oh, good idea!" Jessica said approvingly. "She can come get us and take you to the hospital."

But after twenty rings Bruce had to admit defeat. Lila wasn't going to answer. She'd even turned off her answering machine. "She's not home," he said bitterly, hanging up the phone. "She's *never* home when I need her."

Even as he said it, he knew it wasn't fair. *I should have skipped Professor Gordon's class that day I found the flowers on her porch*, he realized sadly. *I should have waited for her to come home so we could have worked everything out before—*

Wait a minute—the florist! Bruce had taken Marcus's card out of the bouquet—he knew which florist Marcus had used. The shop was the closest one to campus.

"Come on," Bruce told Jessica, walking quickly out of the gas station parking lot.

"Where are we going?" Jessica asked, trotting along at his side.

"To get a car."

"Where?"

Bruce didn't answer as he walked back in the direction of Crestview. He'd seen a little wooded park near the base of the hill just a few blocks away. It would be the perfect place.

"I don't understand," Jessica protested as they reached the edge of the park. "What are we doing here?"

"You'll see." The park was as dark as Bruce had hoped it would be, and he strode quickly across the grass toward the parking area. There were several cars parked on the hard-packed

181

dirt, but no people in sight. "Keep an eye out. Let me know if you see anyone coming."

"You're not going to steal a car!" Jessica admonished him, horrified. "Let's just take a cab back to campus and get my Jeep."

He was dying, and Jessica was worried about a stupid car! "Just tell me if anyone's coming," Bruce repeated grimly, trying the handle on the nearest door. He didn't have time for a cab or the Jeep—every second counted now.

The first door was locked, so Bruce worked his way down the row. On the fourth car he got lucky. The driver's door was unlocked on an old, beat-up sedan—the kind he remembered how to hot-wire from his hell-raising high-school days. Kneeling in the dirt, Bruce leaned inside and worked frantically underneath the dashboard, his hands trembling and his only illumination coming from the dome light overhead.

"This is a really bad idea," Jessica hissed, shifting her weight noisily. But after a couple of minutes she stopped shuffling and squatted down beside him, watching carefully. "Say, Bruce, um . . . how exactly *do* you hot-wire a car?" she asked curiously. "I mean, not like *I'd* ever do it or anything, but you know . . ."

Bruce suppressed a snort. As much as Jessica Wakefield wanted to pretend she was on higher moral ground than he, she just couldn't resist giving in to temptation. "Forget it, Jessica. I'm almost finished." He breathed a sigh of relief as the engine coughed to life. "Get in," he ordered, climbing up into the driver's seat and unlocking the passenger side.

"All right!" Jessica breathed in apparent awe, running around the car and jumping in without hesitation.

Bruce guided the stolen vehicle quietly out of the parking lot, switching on the headlights only after he'd reached the road. Several miles passed, and Bruce found himself squinting. His vision was more blurred than ever, and the on-coming headlights dazzled his eyes. Despite his best efforts to stay in his lane, the lane markers kept thudding under his drifting tires. He cursed himself for not turning over the wheel to Jessica, but there was no time to stop now.

"I can't believe I'm in a stolen car," Jessica exclaimed, her face revealing a combination of anxiety and forbidden thrill.

"Look, I wouldn't have done this if my life didn't depend on it," he explained. "When this is all over, I'll return it, plus pay damages."

If I live. . . . Bile raged up in Bruce's stomach.

"Jessica, if I . . . uh . . . if something else happens, *you* can call the police and explain. My fingerprints are on the wheel. My . . . my estate can pay for everything."

Jessica seemed to be weighing his words in her head. "You're not going to die, Bruce. But let's go to the hospital. Please." Her eyes were pleading.

"After this next stop."

They drove the rest of the distance to the florist's shop in silence. After her reaction to his taking the car, Bruce didn't want to know how Jessica would react when she found out he was planning to break into the florist's and steal Marcus's address.

Bruce pulled up in the alley behind the shop, trying to remember how it was set up. He'd been inside the shop before, but his recollection of the layout was hazy. *Everything* was hazy. Was the poison affecting his memory now?

He pulled the car up close to the back of the building, a short distance from the florist's wrought-iron security door. To his surprise, a rectangle of light shone through the gate. Someone was working very late.

"What are we doing *here?*" Jessica demanded, irritation in her voice. "I thought we were going to the hospital."

"Marcus bought flowers from this shop to send to Lila," Bruce explained.

Jessica looked at him in disbelief. "Lila! How does she know Marcus?" Then something in Jessica's eyes seemed to click. "So Lila and *Marcus . . . ,*" she said slowly, a sly smile spreading over her features. "Are they . . . ?"

"I don't know, and I don't want to know,"

Bruce cut her off. "But right now we have to get Marcus's address. It might be in their customer files."

"No one's going to let you in this late," Jessica protested. "No offense, but you look scary." She glanced down at their dirty clothes. "We both do."

"We're lucky someone's even here. Besides, you're the fast talker, Jessica. You talk them into letting us in. Then, while you distract the clerk, I'll look through the files."

Jessica gazed at him skeptically. "I'm good, but I don't know if I'm *that* good."

"Oh, come on," Bruce pleaded. "You *know* you are. You're the best."

Jessica smiled and tossed her blond hair. "Of course I am," she agreed. "I just wanted to hear you say it."

The two of them got out of the hot-wired car, leaving it running, and walked to the security door. Through the gate a middle-aged woman could be seen working busily in a large room, fussing with a couple of enormous flower arrangements. There was a litter of discarded cut stems and ribbon scraps everywhere, but the woman didn't seem to be bothered by the mess as she hummed along with an oldie on the radio.

"Excuse me," Jessica called through the narrow bars. "Hi."

The woman jumped, then recovered herself, smiling as she came to the door. "You surprised me," she said, a measure of relief in her voice.

"I'm sorry," Jessica replied. "We didn't mean to. I'm really sorry to bother you, but could we possibly buy a bouquet?"

"Now?" The woman looked at them both as if they were crazy. "At this time of night?"

"You're still here," Bruce pointed out.

The woman smiled and nodded ruefully. "There's a huge order to fill for a wedding tomorrow. I'm afraid I underestimated how long all these arrangements were going to take. I'm going to have to turn you down on that bouquet, though. We're closed." She began walking away from the door.

"Please!" Jessica called at her back. "I know we look awful, and I can see why you don't want to let us in, but we've had such a terrible night. It's . . . uh, our parents' anniversary, and we were on our way to their party when our car broke down. We . . . we tried cutting through some fields to get to a gas station, but it was dark and we got totally lost." She gestured at their dirty clothing, her ruined shoes. "We've missed the party now, but we really wanted to bring our parents something."

The woman hesitated.

"It's their *twenty-fifth* anniversary," Jessica added, pouring on the pathos. "All their friends were supposed to be there. They must be so upset that we never showed up, and we can't disappoint them. *Please?*"

Bruce stood behind her, trying not to let his admiration show. It was inspired lying, even for Jessica.

"You poor things!" the shopkeeper exclaimed, unlocking the door. "Come on in. I guess I can take a few minutes to make you a little bouquet."

She led them through the workroom and up to the front of the shop, where the flowers she had for sale were displayed in a special, glass-fronted refrigerator. "Now what would you like for your parents?" she asked Jessica.

"Oh, everything's so pretty," Jessica stalled. "Let me see." Jessica kept the woman busy with a flurry of questions and appeals for advice while Bruce looked nervously around him, trying to guess where the customer files were. After a few frantic minutes his gaze finally landed on a file box next to the cash register. Bruce knew he'd found what he was looking for.

"I like the yellow roses, sis," he said. "Aren't those Mom's favorite?"

"The yellow roses *are* nice . . . ," Jessica said, as if she actually couldn't make up her mind.

"Everyone likes yellow roses," the florist assured them, the tiniest note of impatience in her voice. "Why don't we just take a dozen of these in back and wrap them up with some fern and some nice baby's breath?" She was already pulling the long-stemmed flowers out of the water.

"OK. That sounds perfect," Jessica agreed, following the woman back into the other room.

Bruce lagged behind until the shopkeeper was out of sight, then immediately approached the card file and turned to S. *Stanton, Stanton,* he said to himself as he flipped through the three-by-five-inch index cards. He could hear Jessica chatting up the florist in the other room, but at any moment it was going to occur to the woman that he wasn't there. *Stanton!* Bruce quickly removed the card containing Marcus's information, glancing at it only long enough to see it contained an address other than Lila's. Urgently he stuffed it into his jeans pocket and rejoined the women. The florist didn't seem to have noticed a thing.

"Those are so pretty!" Jessica squealed. "Aren't they pretty, Andrew?"

Apparently he was Andrew now. "Yes. Thank you," Bruce told the florist.

In another minute the woman had the roses all bundled up and tied with a yellow ribbon. "Here you go, sweetie," she said, handing them to Jessica.

"How much do we owe you?" Jessica asked.

"Forget about it," the woman said. "I've already closed the register."

"No, we insist." Bruce opened his wallet—thank goodness he hadn't lost *that*—and laid a hundred-dollar bill on the florist's worktable. "Thanks for everything. Come on, sis."

"Oh, my," Bruce heard the woman breathe as

they darted for the door. "I should say thank *you*."

"Did you get it?" Jessica whispered as soon as they reached the old sedan.

"Got it," Bruce answered. "Thanks . . . you were great." A chill passed through him as he felt his body going limp. He slumped against the still-running car.

"Are you OK?" Jessica asked urgently. "What's wrong?"

"I'm wiped out," Bruce moaned. "Look, Jessica—you'll have to drive us to Marcus's place. I have the address right—"

"Oh no, we're not going to Marcus's." Jessica pushed him in the passenger side and jumped in the driver's seat. "We're going to the hospital. Maybe Dr. Martin's found the antidote and has been trying to beep you. If not, I can call the police from there and let them handle Marcus."

"You're right," he said weakly as Jessica peeled out of the parking lot. Who knew— maybe Dr. Martin *would* have an antidote. But if not, Bruce had no intention of wasting any more time with the police. And he wasn't planning to hang around watching the clock run out at the hospital either.

"OK," Jessica said urgently as she pulled into a space outside the hospital emergency room. "We're here. Let's go."

"Listen, Jessica, do me a favor," Bruce

slurred. "Go in and find Dr. Martin. Then come out and get me with a wheelchair or stretcher or something. I don't feel well enough to walk all over the hospital right now."

"Sure. No problem." He sure didn't *look* well enough. His skin was pasty white, and the circles under his eyes were almost as dark as his hair. "Stay here," Jessica told him. "I'll be right back."

"Don't stop until you find Dr. Martin," Bruce pleaded as she bolted for the emergency-room doors.

Jessica gasped when she saw the clock over the reception area—eleven-thirty. Almost midnight already! She prayed that the doctor had already identified the poison as she approached. "I need to speak to Dr. Martin, please; it's urgent," Jessica told the receptionist. "Tell her it's about Bruce Patman."

He nodded and called for the doctor over the intercom. Moments later a woman in a white lab coat burst purposefully into the reception area.

"Dr. Martin?"

"How's Bruce?" the doctor asked impatiently. "Is he . . . ?"

"No," Jessica replied. "But he's very weak. He's in the parking lot, waiting in the car. Do you have the antidote yet?"

Dr. Martin shook her head sadly, but the expression on her face remained determined. "Not yet. But we haven't given up, and neither should Bruce."

"He hasn't. He wants to check himself in."

Dr. Martin nodded. "That's probably the best thing at this point. He must be in terrific pain. Drive him up to the doors and we'll get a wheelchair."

Jessica turned and ran back out to the still-running car. Bruce looked even worse than when she had left him. His breathing was labored, and his skin was clammy.

"Do they have the antidote?" he asked hopefully.

"No, but—"

The idling engine roared unexpectedly. Suddenly Jessica realized that Bruce had moved into the driver's seat while she was inside the hospital. She barely had time to step backward and save her toes as Bruce peeled out of the parking lot.

"Bruce Patman! You *idiot!*" she screamed in frustration at the sedan's taillights. "You're going to kill *yourself!*"

"That doesn't look like a palace of the rich and famous to me," Bruce muttered as he pulled up quietly outside Marcus's home. "Please, don't let this be a fake address." He had been thankful for the rest he'd had while Jessica drove—his vision had improved slightly, and sheer willpower and adrenaline had helped him keep control of the car through the twists and turns through Crestview. But now he was afraid his efforts were all for nothing.

The neighborhood was pure cracker box; the houses were the kind that had been built in the Dark Ages for temporary housing and then had been considered too unimportant to even bother taking down. It was the type of neighborhood the old Bruce wouldn't have driven his Porsche through on a dare. But the new Bruce was desperate and driving a stolen car.

Marcus's shack was smaller than the surrounding houses but on a bigger parcel of land, with a vacant lot behind it. Even in the dark Bruce could see that the yard was poorly kept and overrun with weeds, and the decrepit wooden siding looked as if it hadn't been painted since the place was new. Bruce pulled the florist's card from his pocket and double-checked the address, praying that he'd find Marcus inside. Finally he got out of the car quietly, leaving the car door open.

With a single nervous glance up and down the deserted street, Bruce crept up the walkway. The house was dark. Reaching the door, Bruce put his ear to the wood to listen. Very faintly he heard the sound of a television. He listened a few more seconds, then, hearing nothing else, tried the doorknob. To his surprise, the door was unlocked. Bruce pushed the door open carefully, quietly, hoping to catch Marcus by surprise. The door opened only an inch, though, before it was caught by a security chain. So much for catching Marcus unawares.

Bruce peered through the crack into the interior. The room in front of him was dark and sparsely furnished. Over to the right he could see the rising and falling light of a television set spilling through a bedroom door, and at the back of the tiny house, beyond the front room, a dim light illuminated the kitchen. Bruce took a deep breath, stepped back from the door, then threw his entire weight into the decaying wood.

The chain gave way and the door flew open, slamming into the adjacent wall. Bruce stumbled forward into the main room, trying desperately to regain his balance on feeble legs. Pain from his impact with the door made the room swim around him, and spots returned, clouding his vision. Then suddenly the room was flooded with light, nearly blinding him. Marcus stood in a doorway on the opposite side of the room, dressed only in a pair of ragged sweatpants, a frightened expression on his face.

"You!" he gasped, staring at Bruce.

Bruce lunged at Marcus, grabbing him by the neck. "You'd better tell me what you poisoned me with! *Now!*"

Marcus's eyes darted toward the door as if measuring his escape. Then his hands jabbed up between Bruce's weak arms, easily batting them away. With a push that sent Bruce reeling backward, Marcus ran for the open front door. Instinctively Bruce stuck out a leg and tripped him. Marcus went sprawling, hitting his head on a coffee table as he went down. After struggling to his feet Bruce walked over and pushed the door closed.

"Now you're going to tell me everything," Bruce said, his voice low and menacing. "If you're so rich, how come you're living in this dump? What kind of scam are you trying to pull?"

Marcus closed his eyes briefly, as if he hoped that would make Bruce go away. But when he opened them again, Bruce was still waiting. "It doesn't have anything to do with you," Marcus managed.

"Nothing to do with me?" Bruce hollered in disbelief. "You murder Belinda Beringer, you *poison* me, and now you're pretending to be rich and move in on my girlfriend? That's got nothing to do with me?"

Marcus looked alarmed. "You have it all wrong. I don't even know what you're talking about."

"Get up," Bruce ordered. He tried to haul Marcus to his feet but found he wasn't strong enough—his waning energy had been spent when he broke through the door—and Marcus remained stubbornly on the carpet. "I don't have time for these games, and you know it," Bruce shouted angrily. "Now get up and tell me the antidote!"

"The antidote?" Marcus repeated blankly, rising slowly and brushing himself off. "You're not making sense."

With an enraged roar Bruce shoved Marcus backward over the coffee table. Only then did Bruce see what was lying on the table in plain sight—the missing pink-and-white copy of his screenplay.

"Oh, so you don't know what I'm talking about," Bruce mocked viciously, lifting *The Victim* off the table. "You liar! What are you doing with my screenplay?" Without waiting for an answer Bruce flung himself at Marcus and grabbed his neck again, this time in a firm choke hold. He could feel the heat of Marcus's flesh radiating up through his hands as his fingers gripped tighter, tighter. If only he were stronger! Bruce put his full body weight behind his arms, trying to compensate for his increasing weakness. "You'd better start talking," he warned. "Because if you don't, I don't have a reason in the world not to kill you for what you've done to me."

"I . . . I found it in the library," Marcus choked. "I was just curious."

Bruce glared down at him, his eyes narrowing with angry disbelief.

"It's brilliant," Marcus added desperately. "You . . . you should be careful who you show it to."

Bruce became possessed with sarcastic laughter. "No kidding! If you hadn't read it, you wouldn't have known how to poison me."

"I read your script, but I didn't *poison* you," Marcus insisted, his hands struggling to pry Bruce's from his throat. "I'd never do something like that."

"Tell that to Belinda Beringer."

"No! You've got it all wrong!"

"Then straighten me out," Bruce suggested, losing patience. He pushed down harder on Marcus's neck. "Now! Or I swear I'll kill you."

Marcus's eyes looked frantic, as if he believed Bruce would carry out his threat. "Look, I did take the money in Belinda's trust fund, but I didn't kill her. I loved her!"

"Keep trying," Bruce advised, applying more pressure.

"Someone else killed her," Marcus gasped desperately. "I swear."

"Then where's the money?" Bruce demanded, lightening up on Marcus's throat enough to let him speak. "You don't expect me to believe you've got Belinda's money and *want* to live here."

"I . . . it's . . . gone. I was going to produce Belinda's last screenplay with the money, but the script was missing after she died," he explained. "So I bought the car, some clothes . . . paid for tuition. But I lost the rest of it gambling. It's the truth."

"You don't fool me," Bruce spat. "You took all her money and killed her!" He tightened his grip on Marcus's throat again slowly, methodically. "Is that what you were planning to do to Lila too?"

"Li-Lila?" Marcus sputtered. "How . . . do . . . you . . . know . . . Lila?"

Bruce dug his thumbs deep into the tender flesh at the base of his enemy's throat, causing

Marcus's brown eyes to bulge. "You knew she was my girlfriend all along," he accused. "Why else would you try to kill me? You had to get me out of your way."

Marcus's hands clawed weakly at Bruce's, trying to pry them away. "You're . . . you're *crazy!*" Marcus choked out through clipped gasps. He struggled underneath Bruce, then stiffened, then relaxed.

Apprehensively Bruce released his hands from Marcus's neck, bending to check his glassy, unseeing eyes. "Oh no," Bruce breathed as he realized what he'd just done. "Oh no!"

Things had gone too far, too fast. Marcus was dead. Panic flooded Bruce's system with adrenaline, making him nauseous. Not only had he just killed Marcus, he'd just killed himself! With Marcus dead, how would Bruce ever find the antidote?

Then with a tremendous, unexpected push Marcus sent Bruce hurtling backward. Bruce felt the edge of the coffee table crack him across his spine as Marcus scrambled off the floor and headed for the kitchen.

In spite of the pain exploding in his back Bruce staggered to his feet and ran after Marcus. He caught him in the kitchen just before he slipped out the back door. The two of them struggled wildly, smashing into the walls, the kitchen counter, the tiny dinette and its two flimsy chairs. Bruce did his best, but he was rapidly losing the fight. It had taken all the strength he had to get the better of Marcus the first time around—now there was nothing left.

Marcus seemed to sense this as he gave Bruce a last, desperate push that sent Bruce sprawling into the dinette. Bruce grasped hysterically at the furniture as he went down, but the cheap little table was too light to afford him any anchor—instead he pulled it down on top of him. Bruce watched helplessly from the floor as Marcus snapped back the bolt and opened the kitchen door, revealing the night sky. He was about to get away!

"No! Wait!" Bruce called weakly, trying to get to his feet. "Please!"

Marcus hesitated at the door and suddenly turned back, his eyes wide with surprise, then fear. He bolted toward a drawer in the kitchen, fumbling desperately for something inside.

A gun.

"No!" Bruce shouted.

Marcus swung the gun around, poised to shoot.

"No!" Bruce yelled again, just as the gunshot sounded.

Then everything faded away.

Chapter Twelve

"I want to report a murder," Bruce told the 911 operator, gripping the telephone with both trembling hands. From where he stood, he could still see Marcus in the kitchen, a pool of blood spreading out rapidly on the grimy linoleum around him. He was dead—a bullet in his brain and an unfired gun clutched in his stiffening hand.

"Who am I speaking with?" the operator asked.

"Look, never mind about that," Bruce snapped, shivering uncontrollably. "Just send someone over here. One-two-seven-four West Fiftieth."

"I'll need more informa—"

Bruce hung up. The police could come or not—it didn't really matter. There was nothing they could do for Marcus, and whoever had killed him was gone.

When Bruce had recovered from his faint, the house had been dark and silent. At first he'd thought he was dead, that Marcus had shot him. But the familiar pain coursing through his body had gradually convinced him otherwise. He wasn't dead. Not yet.

With a nearly superhuman effort Bruce had managed to push the dinette off him and stand. It was only then that he'd seen Marcus's lifeless body.

As if in a dream Bruce had forced himself to walk outside, to check both the front and back yards. But Marcus's assailant was nowhere to be seen. The killer had disappeared. Stumbling back into the house, Bruce had found the only clue the murderer had left—taken, actually.

His pink-and-white screenplay was gone.

"I've got to get out of here," he muttered, shaking his head as he hurried down the walkway to the car. The time he had left to live was waning, and nothing made any sense. He no longer believed that Marcus had poisoned him, but if not Marcus, then who? Who would want him dead? Bruce's only suspect had been shot right before his eyes, and he hadn't caught even a glimpse of the killer.

Shaken and confused, Bruce guided the black sedan down the dark streets of Marcus's neighborhood. "Try to remember everything you've had to eat or drink in the last twenty-four hours," he instructed himself aloud, trying to regain control of the situation. At the thought of food Bruce's stomach threatened to revolt, but he pushed ahead. "There was the beer at the Blue Lagoon. Then more beer at Jack's party." Bruce paused to wonder briefly if he'd eaten anything at the party. "All I had was toast today," he continued. "And that coffee at the police station. Oh, and that coffee Lila brought over . . ."

That morning's giant plastic-foam cup of coffee loomed suddenly in his vision, larger than life. Now that he thought about it, it was pretty amazing that Lila had gone to so much trouble after everything he'd done to make her hate him. *Unless* . . . no. Bruce shook his head violently, trying to clear the unwelcome suspicions forming there. Lila? No, Lila could *never* do something like this. She loved him. . . .

Yes, she could *have done it,* another part of his brain argued. *After all, she's furious with you. And she had a copy of the screenplay* . . .

No, it was insane. He knew Lila was angry, but she wasn't nuts. If only she'd never gotten mixed up with Marcus! Who knew what kind of lies Marcus had put into Lila's head? And Marcus had killed Belinda . . .

"It's not Lila!" Bruce said out loud.

If not Lila, then who? his thoughts whispered back.

He didn't have an answer.

"Please, not Lila," he prayed, turning the sedan in the direction of her apartment. "Lila would never do this to me. She *wouldn't.*"

Would she?

"Lila?" The door of her apartment was ajar, yet the interior was dark and silent.

No answer.

Bruce pushed the unresisting door open and stepped inside, fumbling for the light switch. He flipped the switch, and cold light flooded the apartment. "Lila?" he called into the empty living room.

Lila would never go out and leave the door open, even for a second—not at this hour, Bruce thought. He walked cautiously farther into the room, wondering what Lila was up to.

Then something odd caught his attention. There was a strange smell in the living room—a hint of smoke. Bruce glanced toward the fireplace. Something had been burning there recently. He crossed to the old stone mantel with a growing sense of dread. Picking up a poker, Bruce opened the wire screen and stirred the ashy remnants in the fireplace.

Someone had been burning paper. A lot of paper. The stack had been so thick that here and there Bruce found a scrap that hadn't been consumed by the blaze. It was pink. Someone had burned a copy of his screenplay in Lila's fireplace. And the ashes were cold, so cold that the copy must have been Lila's.

Bruce's heart started racing with fear. Had Lila burned it herself?

Or was the killer after her too?

"Lila?" he cried, his voice loud and panicked. The ringing of a gunshot echoed in his muddled head, and the sight of Marcus facedown in a pool of blood swam up before him. *No. Not Lila too.*

Bruce rushed through the living room and into her bedroom. Nothing. He was wheeling back around to check the kitchen when he saw a pair of feet protruding through the bathroom doorway, still and lifeless in their ultra-high heels. "Lila!" He ran to her, dropping to the floor at her side and dragging her up off the cold tile into his lap. She lay pale and motionless, unresponsive in his arms.

"Oh no," Bruce cried. "No!" Tears clouded his vision as he held her to him tightly, desperately. She didn't move, didn't wake. She was dead.

"Please, not Lila," he howled, burying his wet face in her hair. "No. Nooo!" He squeezed her tighter, his heart contracting in agony as he rocked back and forth on the floor, not believing it was true.

But gradually Bruce realized something. Lila was chilled but not cold, still but not stiff.

She wasn't dead.

With a burst of adrenaline Bruce rose to his feet, Lila cradled in his arms. Carefully, gently, he brought her to her bed, placed her there carefully, and covered her with a blanket. Then he snatched up her telephone and called 911 for the second time that night.

"Send an ambulance to four-three-five

Goldstream Way immediately," he barked at the 911 operator. "My girlfriend's dying!"

"And what is your name please, sir?"

"Bruce Patman. Hurry!"

"And what exactly is the nature of the problem with your girlfriend?"

"How would I know?" Bruce exploded with fear and impatience. "I just found her on the floor half dead. Now hurry!" He clicked off the cordless phone and threw it away from him, then dropped to the bed at Lila's side.

"Lila?" he whispered. "Lila, can you hear me?"

Lila didn't move. With a gentle hand Bruce smoothed her thick brown hair away from her face, arranging it in a halo on the pillow around her. He found a huge, deep purple lump near her hairline, and Bruce touched a finger to it gingerly. Something—or someone—had knocked her out cold. Bruce pulled a lock of Lila's hair down to cover her injury, letting it sweep gracefully across her white forehead. She was so beautiful but so very, very pale.

As he waited for the paramedics Bruce became overtaken by memories of Lila's smile, her laugh. They swept over him as he sat by her side and held her hand, wanting to comfort her even though she couldn't see or hear him. *Maybe she can*, he realized, entwining her frail fingers with his. "Li," he whispered, leaning over and stroking her hair with his other hand. "Lila, do you have any idea how happy you've made me? How much I love you? I hope you know, because . . . I may not be around to tell you. You're everything to me, Lila. You're more precious than my own life."

What there was left of it. Tears sprang to Bruce's eyes again as he realized that this could be the last time he ever saw her. He might even die not knowing if Lila was going to be OK. Within the next few hours one or both of them would probably be dead. And he'd never know why.

"The ambulance is on its way, Li," he whispered through his tears. "Just hang in there, OK? Please don't die." Lila remained completely motionless, and Bruce felt sick.

Where are the paramedics? Why don't they hurry? he worried, checking his watch. Time had been flying away too quickly ever since the moment he realized he was dying, but now, for him, time seemed suspended, strangely unimportant. Bruce held Lila's cold hand and ignored the precious seconds ticking away. Even if they were his last, he wanted to spend them with Lila. No matter what happened to him, he wasn't going to leave Lila's side until he knew she was going to be all right.

But after that, then what? What would he do next? Where else could he go? Bruce was no closer to finding his killer now than he'd ever been. If anything, things looked bleaker than before. Marcus was dead, and Lila . . .

Oh, Lila, how could I ever have suspected you? he said silently, not wanting to say it out loud—not when Lila was so helpless. Sickening, gut-wrenching guilt overwhelmed him as he gazed at her innocent face. Bruce knew it was his fault that Lila had been attacked—he didn't understand how, but it was.

"I'm sorry, Lila," he leaned down to whisper in her ear. "For everything . . ."

The wail of a siren finally cut the night, and moments later there was a sound of footsteps on Lila's porch. "We're in here!" Bruce shouted, not wanting to leave Lila for even a second. Two paramedics hurried into the room, making the space seem suddenly small.

"What happened?" demanded the first one, motioning Bruce aside and taking Lila's pulse.

"There's a lump on her forehead," Bruce answered. "I found her out cold on the bathroom floor." He knew he should tell them he suspected an attacker, but if the paramedics called the police, Bruce would almost certainly end up being questioned. And that would be a death sentence.

"She must have fallen," the paramedic said. "This kind of thing happens all the time." He examined the bump on Lila's forehead, then looked her over quickly for other signs of injury. "How did she get on the bed?" he asked.

"I carried her," Bruce answered.

The paramedic raised his eyebrows. "You're

lucky you didn't make things worse. Never move the victim." The medic barked some orders at his partner, and the second man went to retrieve the rolling stretcher, but Bruce barely heard him. *"Never move the victim"* echoed loudly in his head.

The Victim.

Bruce was the victim. Then Marcus. Now Lila too? Why would someone go after them?

"OK, let's get her on the stretcher," the lead paramedic said, breaking into Bruce's thoughts. "One, two, up!" The two paramedics transferred Lila skillfully onto the stretcher, which they'd adjusted to the same height as her bed. "Good. Let's roll."

The men began wheeling Lila toward the door almost before Bruce realized what was happening. "Wait!" he called, running after them. "Is she going to be OK?"

The second man turned. "I think so," he said. "We can't say for sure until she's conscious, but her pulse is strong. Things look pretty good."

"Thanks," Bruce gasped, his legs buckling beneath him. It was only then that he realized he'd been holding his breath.

And suddenly Bruce knew what he had to do. He had to stay with Lila. He wanted to be there when Lila woke up, wanted to hold her hand and speak to her one last time, to reminisce about all the things they'd done together, all the dreams they'd shared for the future. He'd wanted to spend his future with Lila—and he still could. All that was left of it now was a couple of hours.

"I'm going with you," Bruce announced to the paramedics.

There was a man. It had to have been a man. What did he want? Something . . . no, nothing. He didn't want anything, but he chased me. Chased me and grabbed me, fought with me. But I escaped. Didn't I? I must have—he's not here now.

Lila held herself perfectly still and listened. She didn't want the man to find her if he was still around.

No, he's not here now. But why is it so hard to open my eyes?

"Lila!"

Bruce's face, just inches from hers, came and went quickly, blinking in and out. *Why? Oh, wait, I'm blinking. I never thought blinking could be this exhausting.*

"Lila, you're awake!"

Her eyelids dropped shut again. *Too heavy.* Of course, that was it. She'd been asleep. She'd had a bad dream, and Bruce was waking her up now. Everything was fine. But what was that funny motion? Was she sick?

Reluctantly Lila opened her eyes again, forcing them to focus on her surroundings. Dimly seen objects streamed by in the darkness on either side of her, as if the bed were rolling. Lila almost panicked, but then she saw Bruce's familiar, reassuring face again. Only who was that stranger at the foot of her bed? And why was her bed *outside?*

"Oh, Lila. Thank God you're OK," Bruce exclaimed, squeezing her shoulder through the blanket. "If anything had happened to you . . ." His voice broke off emotionally.

What is he talking about? With an effort Lila thought back. At first nothing came, but then the dull throbbing pain in her forehead helped her remember. It *hadn't* been a dream. The man in her apartment had been real!

"What happened?" she asked, struggling to sit up. "What happened to me?"

"Please don't try to move, miss," the person at the end of her bed instructed. She realized he was wearing a white uniform.

Am I being hauled off to the funny farm? That's it. I imagined everything. I must be going crazy. . . .

"You're on a stretcher," the man continued. "We're just going to take you to the hospital and get you checked out."

"I found you unconscious in the bathroom," Bruce hurriedly explained. "There's a big lump on your head."

Lila groaned and relaxed back into the stretcher. "I'll bet there is," she said weakly. "I must look awful."

"You look beautiful," Bruce whispered sincerely. "Absolutely beautiful." There were tears in his eyes.

Fear gripped Lila suddenly. "What's wrong?" she demanded. Bruce's expression went beyond tender, beyond relieved—it was haunted, desperate. "I'm not going to make it, am I?" she asked.

"You're going to be fine," a calm voice promised from the head of the stretcher. "OK, let's get her loaded into the ambulance."

"Wait!" Lila struggled to sit, but strong straps held her down. "Please, can I talk to my boyfriend alone for a minute?"

"We've got to get you to the hospital," the paramedic at her feet protested.

"Just one minute," Lila begged. "Please." It hurt to talk—it hurt to *breathe*—but something was seriously wrong. Bruce—long-absent, deeply missed Bruce—would tell her what it was.

The two men hesitated. "All right," the paramedic at her feet agreed at last, "but we aren't supposed to do this. One minute, and that's it." He and his partner drifted off a short distance into the darkness.

"Bruce, what is it?" Lila whispered urgently as soon as they were alone. "What's going on?"

He hesitated, staring down at her face as if he were trying to memorize every feature, every detail. His expression was so intense that it scared her. But even more frightening were the deep purple circles under his glassy blue eyes, the sunkenness of his pale cheeks. He looked like death.

"Bruce, please. You're scaring me," she

whispered. "What's wrong? Is it about the man who attacked me?"

That seemed to snap him out of it. "Lila, are you sure it was a man who attacked you? What did he look like? Did you see *anything*?"

Lila closed her eyes, trying to decide what to say. *I have to tell him about Marcus,* she thought. But the very next instant she changed her mind. Her attacker had been tall, but Marcus was *very* tall. And the voice when she'd stepped on his foot—it was too low, all wrong. The man in her apartment hadn't been Marcus. Lila was sure of it.

"It was a tall man dressed in black. That's all I saw. I was trying to get away when he tripped me, and I hit my head, I think. They didn't catch him?"

Bruce shook his head. "Not yet. Lila, listen to me. Someone is trying to kill me. I know it's hard to believe, but I've been poisoned. I only have two, maybe three more hours to live."

"What!" Again the stretcher straps restrained her. Bruce *dying*? It couldn't be true! But the way he looked, the frail, weak way he moved . . . "Oh no." A cold panic gripped her, pressing down on her chest, suffocating her. "Bruce, this can't be happening!"

"I wish it weren't." He closed his eyes, squeezing them against tears, then opened them again. "I'm just glad you're all right. I . . . I love you so much," he whispered, his voice hoarse with emotion. "I just wanted you to know that."

Lila burst into tears. "I love you too," she sobbed.

He leaned down over her, embracing her on the stretcher. Lila wanted desperately to put her arms around him, but she couldn't move them.

"Remember when I crashed my plane in the mountains?" he asked. "We thought we were both going to die up there in the snow before anyone found us."

Lila nodded through her tears.

"When we survived that, I figured nothing worse could ever happen," he said, a wry half smile on his face. "I never imagined my life would end like this. I . . . I wish I could take back the last few weeks, Lila, and—"

"Stop it! Stop it—don't say that!" Lila interrupted, sobs racking her body. "Bruce, you can't die! There's got to be a doctor who can help you!"

Bruce shook his head, his tears falling freely, raining down on her face. "Not without knowing what kind of poison it is," he managed. "And the only person who knows that is probably the same man who attacked you."

"Then you have to catch him," Lila shouted, becoming completely hysterical. "Bruce, you have to find him!"

"OK," a paramedic's voice cut in firmly. "That's enough. We have to get her to the hospital now." He shot Bruce a dirty look as he and his partner began loading Lila's stretcher. "You're agitating the patient."

"I'm not agitated!" Lila screamed. "Bruce! *Bruce!*"

"Don't worry," Bruce said softly, following her into the ambulance. "I'm not going to leave you."

"Yes, you are. You *are!*" she sobbed. "Go find that person *now!*"

"I'm going to ride with you—" Bruce began.

"No. Get out!" Lila demanded. "Please," she added before the tears overwhelmed her.

For several seconds the quiet in the ambulance was broken only by the sound of Lila's ragged sobbing, then Bruce's lips touched hers, perhaps for the last time. She closed her eyes, savoring the sweetness of his kiss, her fear temporarily dissolving into warmth and love. It wouldn't be their last kiss. No, it couldn't be. . . .

"Just remember," Bruce whispered, his breath warm and alive on her ear, "I'll always love you. Forever." His lips brushed her temple. "Please . . . don't forget me, Lila."

"No, don't say that! Nothing's going to happen to you!" she insisted, struggling to see his face. But he wasn't by her side anymore.

"OK. We're out of here," came the lead medic's voice, followed by a harsh slamming of doors at the rear of the ambulance. Bruce was gone. It felt like a black hole in her heart.

Why did I make him go away? Lila asked herself, tears streaming down both cheeks. "Oh,

Bruce," she sobbed as the siren began wailing overhead. "I won't forget you. I'll always love you too. Forever."

The siren faded off into the distance as Bruce walked back to Lila's apartment, still wishing he'd gone with her. What chance did he have to live now anyway? There was no way of knowing who'd attacked Lila, no lead for Bruce to follow. If he'd stayed with her, his final hours could have been happy. Now there was nothing to do but wait.

Wandering into Lila's bedroom, Bruce retrieved the phone from the floor and punched in a number. "Sweet Valley Emergency," answered a tired male voice on the other end.

"Yes, please page Jessica Wakefield," Bruce said. "It's urgent." Bruce had expected an argument or to be told that Jessica wasn't there, but instead she came on the line almost immediately.

"Where are you?" Jessica demanded irately. "And what was that stunt you pulled in the parking lot?" Then, a little less angrily, "Are you all right?"

"As well as can be expected," Bruce answered grimly. "I'm glad you're still there."

"I was hoping you'd get smart and come back," Jessica told him. "Dr. Martin is worried about you. We both are, believe it or not."

"Still no luck?" Bruce asked, already knowing the answer. If Dr. Martin had discovered the antidote, Jessica would have told him immediately.

"No," she admitted. "But they're working at it really hard. Bruce, you have to come back here."

"I wish I could," he said, meaning it. "But Lila wants me to keep trying to find whoever poisoned me."

"Lila?" Jessica sounded confused. "You guys made up?"

"She's on her way to the hospital, Jessica. Someone attacked her."

"No!" Jessica exclaimed, her voice tight and frightened. "Ohmigosh—is she OK?"

"She's going to be fine, but could you track her down and keep an eye on her?"

"Of course," Jessica agreed shakily, her relief evident.

"Call the police too and make a report."

"But Bruce," Jessica protested. "What about you? What are you going to do?"

"I don't know," he answered honestly. "Keep checking with Dr. Martin, all right? If I can, I'll call you later."

"If you *can?*" Jessica repeated, alarmed, but Bruce hung up the phone. His time was almost up— dawn would be breaking soon. Even now a cold, drenching sweat oozed from every pore and chills racked his body. While he had feared for Lila's life, Bruce had somehow managed to ignore the poison in his system, but now he felt the sickness coursing through his veins, ready to take him over completely. His death was so inevitable, he almost welcomed it.

"Let it be over," he whispered, falling backward onto Lila's bed. He could lie there, just lie there until it happened. Bruce closed his eyes, imagining how his corpse would look, stiff and cold on Lila's bedspread. It would be so peaceful to slip out of life this way, surrounded by the scent of Lila's perfume. They'd find his body tomorrow, and maybe someday someone would find out who'd killed him.

Or maybe not.

Bruce forced his eyes open and sat up, shaking his head to clear his clouded vision. He wouldn't give his killer that kind of advantage. For as long as he could, he owed it to himself—and to Lila—to keep trying. He wouldn't just lie down and wait for death to find him. No, he'd fight it to the end. And maybe, just maybe, he'd cheat it.

He was struggling to his feet when a new thought stopped him cold. "Oh no!" he whispered, feeling the panic rise up within him. "Could he . . . no, he couldn't be. But maybe . . ." Immediately he seized the phone up off the floor and punched 411.

"Information," chirped the operator. "What city, please?"

"Sweet Valley," said Bruce. "I need a listing for Dennis Gordon."

Chapter
Thirteen

"Bruce Patman?" the professor's groggy voice repeated at the other end of the line. "Oh sure, Bruce. What's on your mind?"

"I have to talk to you right away," Bruce said urgently. "Can you meet me at your office?"

"Now?" asked the professor. "What time is it anyway?"

Bruce glanced at the clock on Lila's dresser, wincing at what he saw. "Almost four in the morning. I wouldn't ask if it wasn't an emergency."

"An emergency?" Professor Gordon seemed a little more awake. "That sounds pretty serious. Can't we discuss it on the phone?"

Bruce hesitated. "No. I need to see you in person," he said. "Please. Can't you meet me in your office?"

"Sure, Bruce," Professor Gordon agreed slowly. "If you're sure it's really necessary."

"It is," Bruce said quickly. "How fast can you be there?"

"Well, you woke me up. I'll have to shower and get dressed and—"

"Don't shower!" Bruce interrupted. "There's no time. Just come as quickly as you can!"

"All right, then, Bruce," the professor said. "I'll see you in my office as soon as humanly possible."

"Thank you!" Bruce exclaimed, momentarily relieved. He hung up the phone and headed for Lila's front door.

There was only one thing Bruce knew for sure anymore: Whoever had poisoned him had read *The Victim*. The way he'd been poisoned had made him suspect it, but the fact that some crazed psycho had stolen Marcus's copy and burned Lila's made him certain.

And now there was only one copy of the screenplay left—the professor's. And he had to talk to him before it was too late.

Bruce let himself into Professor Gordon's office, looking around a second before he sank, disoriented, into one of the plush leather chairs facing the desk. He'd driven his stolen sedan to campus, but the long walk to the professor's office from the parking lot had taken every ounce of strength he'd had. He shook his head, trying to quiet the now incessant roar in his ears, but the movement only stirred up those silver spots again. They floated before his eyes as thickly as snowflakes in a blizzard.

"Where is he?" Bruce muttered impatiently. He'd contacted the professor with no real agenda, unsure what the visit would prove. All he knew was that Professor Gordon might know something—anything—about what was going on. It was a slim hope, Bruce knew, but it was the only hope he had. If nothing else, Bruce could warn the professor that his name could be next on the killer's list.

Bruce checked his watch: four-thirty. The sun would come up in another hour or so. Already the sky outside the professor's window seemed lighter, and Bruce prayed it was only his imagination.

He thought back to the dawn he'd watched break over Sweet Valley on Monday, when he'd finished *The Victim*. It seemed now like something he'd done in another lifetime. He'd been foolish enough to be proud of his screenplay then; he'd been so sure that the problems between him and Lila could be fixed with a quick apology and a fancy dinner. His entire life had been ahead of him then. Now it was gone.

Bruce turned his left wrist toward his face to double-check the time and noticed that his hand—his entire arm—was shaking violently. He watched it with an odd sort of detachment.

"You're not going to make it, Patman," he said out loud. His words sounded thin behind the roaring in his ears. Even if Professor Gordon did come through with some information, Bruce didn't think he had the strength to do anything about it anymore.

"Face it. You're going to die." The thought made him feel lightheaded—lightheaded and strangely giddy. The whole thing seemed so ludicrous. "You're going to croak. Buy the farm. Push up daisies. Make out your will."

Suddenly he had an idea. He *could* make out his will. He didn't have one, and he didn't want his trust fund to be simply absorbed back into his parents' vast fortunes. He wanted his friends to have something. He wanted Lila to have something. Professor Gordon could witness it when he got there—*if* he ever got there.

Using the edge of the professor's desk for support, Bruce pulled himself to his feet. He slowly made his way around the professor's desk to the large leather chair on the other side. He collapsed into it unsteadily, still gripping the desktop. Sitting in the professor's chair seemed a little weird, but his legs were like jelly. With only a second's hesitation Bruce opened the top desk drawer, hoping it would contain paper and a pen, but the sight that met his eyes made him groan.

A thick, ragged screenplay rested inside the drawer, a dirty-looking white cover sheet on top. *The Victim,* it read, *by Bruce Patman.* "That's the last thing in the world I want to see right now,"

Bruce quipped as he pulled it out of the drawer. "Who knows—maybe it will be," he added pessimistically. "I should throw this in the wastebasket where it belongs."

But underneath it was another screenplay, this one looking crisp and perfect. *The Victim,* proclaimed that gleaming-white cover page, *by Dennis Gordon.*

Bruce felt as if he'd been punched in the stomach. What was this all about? Why would the professor put his own name on a terrible script like *The Victim?* Dennis Gordon was an award-winning screenwriter. He didn't need to steal student scripts. Not only that, but *The Victim* stank. At least that was what the professor had said.

Suddenly another voice echoed in his head. *"It's brilliant,"* he heard Marcus Stanton choke out through the hands—Bruce's hands—closing around his throat. *"You should be careful who you show it to."*

Bruce's heart pounded feverishly as he turned to look at the screenplay in his hand. The first half of it was white, the second half pink. He dropped it on top of the desk involuntarily. "No," he murmured, his eyes searching the office desperately. "It can't be. It *couldn't* be. How could he have . . ."

He trailed off as his gaze fell on the heavy crystal decanter of Scotch glinting in the light of the desk lamp.

•   •   •

"Lila! Are you all right?" Jessica's voice floated down to Lila as if from a great distance.

With great effort Lila opened her eyes. "Jessica," she wheezed, shaking the sleep out of her eyes. "Why are you running?"

Jessica chuckled, waking Lila up enough to realize she was being wheeled on a gurney down a hospital hallway, Jessica trotting alongside her.

"They're taking you to a private room," Jessica said. "And I'm coming with you."

"What are you doing here? Did Bruce call you?"

"Uh-huh. He told me what happened. Oh, Lila, I can't believe it!" she added in a worried rush. "You've got a concussion, but the doctors said you're going to be just fine. I hope the sleazeball who did this gets locked up for life."

"Me too," Lila said softly, memories of her attack and her reconciliation with Bruce coming back to her in waves. *Oh no . . . Bruce.* Tears came to her eyes, and she could hardly believe she had any left. She must have cried herself to sleep a dozen times since leaving him at the apartment. Everything seemed to be a blur, and the pain in her head was unbearable.

"Li, what's wrong?" Jessica asked urgently. "Nurse—"

"No, I'm fine," Lila interrupted. "We—we need to talk, Jess. It's about Bruce."

"I know," Jessica replied softly.

Lila was wheeled into a room with a sharp

turn and helped by the nurse and orderly into the bed. The sheets were cool and smooth, but the comfortable surroundings brought her no pleasure. All she cared about was her boyfriend.

"What do you know about Bruce?" Lila asked Jessica as soon as the orderly left the room. "Do you know about the poison?"

"I know everything," Jessica admitted, her eyes glittering. "What happened when you got attacked?"

Lila groaned and waved one hand impatiently. "Someone grabbed me outside my apartment. I tried to get away, but I fell and hit my head. But that's not important. What about Bruce? Have you talked to him? Is he going to be all right?"

Jessica perched on the edge of the bed. For the first time Lila noticed that Jessica's clothes were wrinkled and dirty, and her usually gorgeous blond hair badly needed brushing. In fact, she looked about as tired and *un*-fabulous as Lila had ever seen her.

"It's bad, Lila," Jessica answered in a low voice. "I won't lie to you. I was already here before you came in, waiting for Dr. Martin to finish the tests on Bruce's blood samples. If the doctor doesn't discover the antidote, or if Bruce doesn't find the killer, Bruce is going to die."

Lila closed her eyes. "I know."

"Bruce hasn't checked in for a while." Jessica

223

squeezed Lila's hand through the covers. "But don't give up, Li. We know how stubborn Bruce is—"

Lila giggled in spite of her sorrow, causing a couple of tears to fall down her cheek.

"—and Dr. Martin could still find the antidote. If she does, I promise you I'll track Bruce down somehow. It's what I've been waiting here to do."

Lila nodded gratefully, and more tears poured out from under her closed eyelids. She still couldn't believe that any of this was happening. Bruce was in danger, was *dying*, and there was nothing she could do to help. She had never felt so useless. Jessica leaned over and hugged her gently, and the tears came even faster.

"Excuse me, ladies," interrupted a gravelly male voice from the doorway. "Is this Lila Fowler's room?"

"I'm Lila," she responded quickly, wiping at her tears with the fingers of both hands.

"Detective Warren," her visitor said. "May I come in?"

"Yes. Please." Lila struggled into a sitting position, and Jessica moved off the bed and into a chair on the other side of the room. Detective Warren strode in, a small spiral pad in his hand.

"My office received a call from a Jessica Wakefield, who—"

"That's me!" Jessica interrupted from her chair, waving.

The detective nodded at Jessica, then returned his attention to Lila. "I understand that you've been injured as the result of an attack on you at your apartment. If you feel up to it, I'd like to ask you a few questions."

"Of course," Lila agreed. "But I'm afraid I'm not going to be much help. It was so dark, I never even got a look at the guy."

"But you believe it was a man?" the detective asked.

"Yes, I'm sure of it," Lila answered.

Detective Warren jotted something in his book. "I understand that you're Bruce Patman's girlfriend and that he made the call for the ambulance. Is that correct?"

Lila felt a momentary flash of surprise, then hope. "Yes, that's right. Do you know where Bruce is now?"

The detective's eyes narrowed. "No. Do you?"

"No, but he's been poisoned. Someone is trying to—"

"I know, I know," Detective Warren interrupted impatiently. "I know the whole story. Are you sure you don't know where he is?"

"I last saw him at my apartment, but I know he's out looking for the person who poisoned him. Please help him, Detective."

The detective rubbed at his bloodshot eyes. "I'm *trying* to help him, but he's not exactly making it easy. I've had an officer stationed at his apartment for hours, but he hasn't come home. You're *positive* that you don't know where he is?"

Lila nodded, and a couple of lingering tears spilled with the motion.

"All right, then. This man who attacked you—is there anything at all you can remember about him?"

Lila strained to remember something, anything, but nothing came back. Only the fear. And the searing, blinding pain as her head collided with porcelain. "Just that he was tall. And dressed in black. I know that's not much—I'm sorry."

"What were you burning in your fireplace tonight?"

"Excuse me?" The question took her completely by surprise.

"We've already been to your apartment. There was a whole lot of paper burned in your fireplace very recently. It appears to have been some type of manuscript."

"A manuscript?" Lila repeated, confused. "I don't . . . wait—was there a screenplay on the living-room table?"

Detective Warren flipped through some notes. "No mention of one here."

"Bruce gave me a copy of a screenplay he'd written. But I didn't burn it—I left it on the table."

"Hmmm," said the detective, writing rapidly. "I'll have someone go back and double-check that. We've recovered a few paper fragments that survived the fire. If it turned out that they belonged to your boyfriend's screenplay, could you identify them?"

"Only by the color," Lila said, feeling utterly useless. "The paper was pink, but I . . . I never read it."

The detective looked at her suspiciously, then seemed to accept the truth of her words. He took a business card from his shirt pocket. "Here's my card," he said, handing it to her. "Call me if you remember anything else at all."

Bruce grabbed the heavy crystal decanter with both hands, his heart pounding with fear and excitement. His entire fate sparkled in the dark amber liquor inside. If Bruce could get the Scotch back to Dr. Martin in time, maybe she'd be able to identify the toxin Professor Gordon had laced it with.

"Now I know why you're not coming," Bruce muttered as if Professor Gordon could hear him. "And that's just fine with me." Even if he did show, Bruce was far to weak too force the professor to tell him what the poison was. No, Bruce's best chance was to get back to the hospital with the Scotch. There was still time for the doctors to save him—there had to be.

He struggled to his feet, almost too weak to keep the decanter from slipping through his fingers and shattering on the floor. He bobbled it once, catching it before it slipped, and his heart pounded so fiercely, he was afraid it would give out at any moment. But as he stumbled toward the door it slammed open and hit the wall with a bang. Bruce froze, his heart pounding. "Professor Gordon," he gasped. "Hi."

Professor Gordon smiled and strode into the office, limping slightly. His friendly green eyes searched Bruce's dimming blue ones as Bruce fumbled desperately with the bottle, trying to hide it behind his back.

"Bruce!" the professor greeted him jovially. "I got here as quickly as I could. Now what's all this cloak-and-dagger urgency about at such an unnatural hour?"

He's bluffing, Bruce thought. *He knows.*

"Have a seat," Professor Gordon offered, closing the door behind him. "I can't wait to hear what you have to tell me."

You have to get out of here, Bruce told himself desperately. *But how?* Professor Gordon still stood in front of the door, blocking Bruce's exit.

"I . . . uh, really appreciate your coming to meet me," Bruce said, wondering if he could fool the professor into believing nothing was wrong. "But, uh . . . the truth is that I don't remember why I called you anymore. I . . . I'm afraid I had a little too much to drink and I . . . uh . . . I had this sudden urge to discuss Fellini.

But I feel better now. I'm sorry to have bothered you."

"Drinking's a bad habit," the professor said slowly. "You of all people should know that by now."

Bruce's eyes met the professor's. The false friendliness that had been there before had vanished. In its place was something vacant, something almost evil.

He's insane, Bruce realized. *Completely psycho.* Sucking in his breath, Bruce rushed for the door.

Professor Gordon sidestepped out of Bruce's path easily, pushing Bruce hard into the still-closed door and snatching the decanter of Scotch at the same time. Bruce crashed into the wood headfirst and slid slowly to the floor.

"Aw, you're not leaving!" Professor Gordon protested, mock joviality in his voice. "Why not have a drink first?" He waved the bottle of Scotch tauntingly over Bruce's head. "It'll cure what ails you," he added in a low, confidential tone. "I'd be happy to pour you a glass."

"I think you've given me enough," Bruce wheezed, his head spinning.

"Oh yes," the professor agreed. "You've had plenty. It's just a matter of time now. And not very much time either, by the look of you."

"You're crazy! You can't possibly believe you're going to get away with this."

The professor smiled and set the decanter

back in its place, taking a seat on the edge of the desk beside it. "Oh, but I already have. I got away with it quite nicely a couple of years ago. Didn't you know that?"

Bruce stared, confused.

Professor Gordon returned Bruce's stare, then threw back his head and laughed. "How rich!" he gasped after a moment. "You really don't know, do you? I would have thought that after all that running around with Marcus—"

"You killed Marcus," Bruce accused dully, clinging to facts that made some sense. "It was you!"

Professor Gordon simply looked amused. "And why would I do that, pray tell?"

Bruce squeezed his eyes shut against the spots that drifted across his vision. He had to think, had to get the professor to confess. If nothing else, maybe he'd be able to escape in time to tell the story to the police and have the professor put away. "You killed Marcus because you wanted his copy of my screenplay," Bruce guessed.

A bark of laughter resounded through the office. "You flatter yourself, Mr. Patman. You really do."

"Oh yeah?" Bruce countered. "Then why was his copy of *The Victim* in your desk?"

The professor glanced back over his shoulder, seemingly noticing the two manuscripts on the desktop for the first time. "Was it?" he asked smugly. "Doesn't look like it's in there now. Are you sure you didn't kill Marcus and bring it here yourself?"

"You know it was," Bruce said. "But what I still don't understand is why. Why did you poison me and shoot Marcus just to steal a student screenplay? You said it wasn't even good."

"Actually," the professor drawled, "the more I thought about it, the less sophomoric I found it. It occurred to me, in fact, that it could even be quite brilliant. With one important change."

"What change?" Bruce demanded.

The professor held up the clean white copy of *The Victim* and pointed proudly to the pristine new cover page. "The author, of course. What else?"

"Try to think, Li," Jessica encouraged her best friend as she sat at her bedside. "Don't you remember anything at all?"

"Nothing useful," Lila insisted. "You have no idea how terrified I was, Jessica. I'm surprised I didn't just stop breathing and make his job easier for him."

"But you struggled," Jessica prompted. "You tried to get away, right?"

Lila's face clouded. "Yes. I stepped on his foot."

"You did? That's good!" Jessica said excitedly. Lila hadn't mentioned that before. "Then what?"

"He . . . uh . . . he yelled and let go of me."

"What did he say?" Jessica pressed.

"I . . . I don't remember."

"Well, what kind of voice did he have?"

Lila shuddered. "Inhuman," she recalled. "I don't think he said anything, actually. He just roared—like an animal in pain."

Jessica raised her eyebrows.

"I was wearing those killer silver heels," Lila explained. "I wouldn't be surprised if I broke his foot or something."

"Lila, that could be important!" Jessica exclaimed. "We have to tell that to the police. What else? What happened next?"

"I don't know," Lila said miserably. "It's all a blur. I was trying to run into the bathroom, and he tackled me. I fell and cracked my head on something. I think I was half out before I actually hit the floor."

"You remember lying on the bathroom floor?" Jessica persisted.

"Barely. I remember the tile felt cool."

"What else?"

"That's all. I passed out."

"Where was the man when you passed out?" Jessica asked.

"I don't know. On the floor too, I guess." Lila reconsidered. "No, wait. He was standing over me. I . . . I remember now."

"What do you remember?" Jessica strained forward on the bed.

Lila started to speak, then wrinkled her forehead, clearly confused. "No," she said, shaking her head. "It must have been a dream."

"What was a dream? *Tell* me!"

"He . . . he said something. But it was so weird. It doesn't make any sense."

"What was it, Li? What did he say?"

"I . . . he . . . he said, 'See you at the movies.'"

Chapter
Fourteen

"See you at the movies?" Jessica repeated, studying Lila's drawn face. "What does that mean?"

Lila sighed and sank back into the pillows. "I don't know," she said. "I already told you it doesn't make any sense. I think I must have dreamed it."

But something about the phrase rankled in Jessica's memory. Hadn't she heard that expression somewhere lately? *See you at the movies,* she repeated to herself. *See you at the movies!*

"Someone said that to me the other day too," she said slowly.

"Who?" Lila asked, her voice surprised.

"I'm trying to remember. . . . Oh, I know. It was Professor Gordon. He wrote it in a copy of *Night Falls Slowly* that I asked him to sign for Elizabeth."

"Oh," Lila said, disappointed. "Well, writing it there makes some sense—unlike saying it to someone you knocked over in a bathroom."

"I guess you're right," Jessica agreed. But then another thought occurred to her. "Lila, what if that *was* Bruce's screenplay in your fireplace?"

"I just don't understand that," Lila moaned. "Why would someone take time out in the middle of attacking me to burn Bruce's stupid screenplay?"

But Jessica barely heard her. The screenplay *had* been written for Professor Gordon's class. The professor *would* have read the script. Not only that, but Professor Gordon had used the same phrase as Lila's attacker. There were too many coincidences to be ignored.

But why would Professor Gordon want Bruce dead?

"Call Detective Warren," Jessica said firmly, rising from the edge of Lila's hospital bed. "Tell him to find Professor Dennis Gordon immediately."

"Jess!" Lila protested. "You don't really think—"

"I don't know what I think anymore," Jessica cut her off. "But I do know that I've got to go." She started for the door.

"Go where?" Lila called from her bed, her voice worried. "What are you doing?"

"Just call that detective," Jessica urged over her shoulder, "and I'll be back as soon as I can."

"What I want to know is *why*," Bruce said, struggling to understand. "Why steal a script from a total unknown?" From his position on the floor Bruce could barely make out the general shape of his killer perched on the edge of the massive desk. The details of his face blurred in and out of Bruce's vision.

"It *is* inconvenient," Professor Gordon admitted cheerfully. "But necessary, I'm afraid. It's unfortunate for you too, of course, but one must do one's part."

By dying? "But you're a *genius!*" Bruce protested. "You won an Academy Award!"

Professor Gordon leaned back a bit, as if savoring that accomplishment, but when he spoke, his voice was cold and bitter. "Ah, yes. *Night Falls Slowly*. A brilliant script."

"That's right!" Bruce agreed. "It was. And you can write another one just as good! Just tell me what you poisoned me with and—"

"Oh, please," the professor interrupted. "You don't really believe I'm so naive, do you?"

"Wha-What do you mean? Everyone says—"

"Idiots, every one. Since you're leaving us anyway, I'll tell you a little secret. I didn't write *Night Falls Slowly*—Belinda Beringer did. And I'm afraid she's not available to help me with the sequel."

"You . . . *you* killed her," Bruce gasped. "It was you, not Marcus!"

"Yes," agreed the professor calmly, folding his hands across his knees. "She made it quite unavoidable. I'd have preferred to keep her around to write my future projects, but writers get so possessive about their little contributions."

Bruce's head was reeling, but he forced himself to concentrate, to keep the professor talking. "Marcus knew you killed her," he said.

The professor moved off the edge of the desk and into the leather chair closest to Bruce. "No. He suspected, of course. But what could the little parasite say after he'd taken all Belinda's money? Marcus was no threat to me—not until you started badgering him for information. It's your fault he's dead, you know."

My fault? Bruce thought, amazed by the professor's ability to rationalize, his total lack of conscience. The thought that this twisted man had once been his hero completely revolted him. "What about Lila?" Bruce demanded. "I suppose that was my fault too."

"Of course," the professor agreed. He was leaning forward in the chair now, and Bruce could finally see his face clearly. "You're the one who gave her a copy of *The Victim.* I can't have copies of my new screenplay floating around all over town, can I?" He laughed. "Someone might say I didn't write it."

"You're sick!" Bruce spat, struggling to stand up against the door. "What kind of psycho kills people over a stupid movie? You should be locked away for life!"

Professor Gordon's eyes narrowed with demented hatred. "I'm sick, am I?" he flung back. "What would a spoiled little rich boy like you know

238

about it? For that matter, what would a spoiled little rich boy like you know about *anything*? Oh, you think you're so smart, with your trust funds and your parties and your fancy cars, but you're nothing—do you hear me? You're *less* than nothing!"

"You're not—" Bruce began angrily.

"Shut up!" Professor Gordon raged. "What do you know about the way the rest of us live? What did Belinda know? Nothing! I'm not sick. People like you *make* me sick—that's the problem."

"That's a—"

"I said *shut up!*" the professor screamed. "I'm tired of your whining. All your life Mommy and Daddy have handed you everything you ever wanted, haven't they? Well, the rest of us haven't had it so good. You think it's easy being a professor? It isn't! All the rules, the stupid university policies, watching people without a tenth of your teaching ability get tenure because they've published some piece of arcane garbage that no one will ever read."

The professor's contorted face had turned virtually purple with fury, and flecks of spit escaped his mouth. "I need your script just to stay alive in this stupid system! One Academy Award isn't enough. No! We must have a sequel! I tell you, it's making me crazy." The professor gripped his head with both hands, as if suddenly in pain. "You're all making me crazy," he moaned. "All I ever wanted to do was teach. I'm a good teacher."

Bruce saw an opportunity and took it. "The best,"

he agreed, forcing sincerity into his sickly voice.

"Be *quiet,* you little worm!" Professor Gordon's head jerked back out of his hands, and his cold eyes glared at Bruce. "What do you know? You're an idiot. Do you hear me? A simple idiot without a brain in your head. You don't deserve to be the author of such a good script! It's mine! *I'm* the one who inspired it—all you did was write down the words. Any moron could have done that. You're stupid, do you hear me? Worthless and *stupid!*"

Rage tore through Bruce, bringing with it a restorative jolt of adrenaline. He could feel his heart pounding more rapidly, furiously, and the spots before his eyes spread into near total blindness as anger forced the blood to Bruce's head. Any pity he might once have been able to feel for his teacher evaporated into loathing as the man continued his tirade.

"Belinda was another story—Belinda had some talent. But you! You're the worst kind of impostor there is! A no-talent hack who thinks he knows it all after only half a class. I'm doing the world a favor, actually, by taking you out of the picture."

With a sudden burst of strength Bruce lunged for the professor. His leather chair toppled with a tremendous crash, and suddenly Bruce was on top of him. Professor Gordon struggled, stunned, as Bruce's hands closed around his throat.

"If you don't tell me what you poisoned me with," Bruce threatened, tightening his grip until the professor's eyes bulged, "you'll die before I do."

Jessica ran out onto the pavement in front of the hospital, waving frantically for a taxi. "Sweet Valley University," she told the driver. "And hurry!"

"You going to the dorms?" the cabbie inquired.

"No, the film school. Can you hurry?"

"OK," he said, pulling away from the curb as Jessica dropped into the backseat. "But no one's going to be there at this hour."

"That's fine," Jessica replied. She was counting on it, in fact. Lila would have called Detective Warren by now, and with any luck the police were already headed to Professor Gordon's house to arrest him. Jessica, on the other hand, was on her way to look for incriminating evidence in his office.

The semidark streets of Sweet Valley slipped by outside the taxi. It was almost dawn. Jessica stared out the window, wishing the light back into darkness for Bruce's sake—and Lila's too.

"You want me to pull in here?" the cabdriver asked, slowing at the entrance to the film-school parking lot.

"No, keep going and drop me at that big building," Jessica directed, pointing up ahead. The taxi passed the parking lot and stopped at the curb closest to the main entrance. Jessica jumped out hurriedly, throwing the driver a twenty-dollar bill she'd managed to tuck inside her bra before Bruce had dragged her out of her dorm room so many hours before.

"Keep the change," she told the driver. Then she turned and sprinted across the deserted pavement toward Professor Gordon's office.

"What do you mean, you don't know where he is?" Lila struggled to keep her voice reasonable. "He was just here a little while ago."

"Detective Warren is off duty now," the police station operator explained. "I can put you through to someone else."

"*No!*" Lila shouted, surprising herself. She took a deep, calming breath. "I mean, Detective Warren already knows all about the case. Can't you page him or something?"

"I can put you through to Detective Finley."

"I don't want to talk to Detective Finley," Lila protested. "I want to talk to—"

"Please hold." The operator's voice cut her off in midsentence.

"I don't want to hold!" Lila yelled into the receiver, only to be greeted by the sound of tinny canned music. She was already holding, whether she wanted to or not.

"Detective Finley," an efficient-sounding female voice answered. "With whom am I speaking, please?"

"This is Lila Fowler. I need to speak to Detective *Warren*. He told me to call him if I remembered anything about my case, and now nobody knows where he is—"

"You can talk to me," Detective Finley interrupted. "I'm working on your case and on your friend Bruce Patman's too."

"Thank goodness!" Lila exclaimed. "Please, you have to find Professor Dennis Gordon right away."

"Dennis Gordon," the detective repeated slowly, as if she were writing down the name. "What for?"

"I think he's involved. In fact, he might even be the person who attacked me."

"Really? What makes you think so?" The detective's voice was calm, but Lila heard the excitement underneath her words.

"It was something he said right as I passed out. He said, 'See you at the movies.'"

"See you at the movies?" the detective repeated skeptically, all the eagerness gone from her tone. "That's it?"

"I know it sounds stupid, but it's a phrase Professor Gordon likes to use. My friend Jessica—"

"All right," Detective Finley broke in. "Don't worry. We'll check him out." But she didn't sound as if it were going to be a priority.

"No, you still don't understand," Lila insisted. "This could save Bruce's life! What if Professor Gordon is also the person who poisoned him?"

There was a brief pause on the other end of the line, then Detective Finley seemed to come to a decision. "All right," she said. "I'll send a car to the professor's house."

"Do it *now*," Lila insisted. "Right away."

"I'll dispatch someone as soon as you let me get off the phone."

Lila hung up and collapsed back into her pillows, tears of fear and frustration coursing down her cheeks. She'd finally made the detective take her seriously, but what if it was already too late?

Bruce glared down into Professor Gordon's reddening face as his fingers squeezed the other man's throat. "I want that antidote," he rasped. "Tell me what poison you used."

The professor shook his head, and Bruce tightened his grip. Then, without warning, the professor pushed violently out from under him, knocking Bruce facedown onto the thick oriental carpet. Before Bruce could recover, the professor was on top of him, straddling his back and pushing his head down against the floor. Bruce fought back, kicking wildly, but his boots met only empty air.

"You didn't really think you'd win, did you?" the professor grunted, forcing Bruce's face into the carpet. "I've wrestled *dogs* that were stronger than you."

Bruce twisted his shoulders against the professor's weight, trying to turn himself faceup, but he couldn't get free. The professor seemed to have suddenly developed incredible strength just at the moment Bruce's own muscles were failing him completely. The adrenaline rush of anger had deserted him, leaving him even weaker and more helpless than before.

"Stop it!" Professor Gordon hissed in his ear. "Don't you know that you're already dead?"

The professor's words, rather than defeating him, spurred Bruce on to struggle harder. If he could just get out of the building with the Scotch, he could still drive to the hospital— could still put his life in Dr. Martin's hands.

"Stop kicking, I said," Professor Gordon ordered, putting a knee on Bruce's back and pressing it down hard into his spine. "I'm sick of your childish behavior."

Bruce struggled to breathe with his face in the carpet while the professor increased the pressure to his spine. The pain was incredible. With a convulsive cry Bruce thrashed away from the tormenting knee, throwing the professor off-balance. With his last ounce of strength Bruce tried to struggle to his feet, but Professor Gordon was too fast for him. Almost as quickly as he'd been knocked off, he was back astride Bruce. Bruce barely managed to flip over in time to be face-to-face with his attacker.

"You ungrateful idiot!" the professor said, his features contorted with anger. "I had everything figured out—all you had to do was lie there and die. Was that so hard? Now I'm going to have to kill you sooner."

His eyes wandered the room, as if casting about for a weapon. "Let's see," he said, almost conversationally. "I could bash your head in with something. That would be messy but effective. I suppose I could throw you out the window." His eyes returned to Bruce and narrowed with annoyance. "If I'd known you were going to be so much trouble, I would have brought my gun."

"Let me go," Bruce gasped. The professor's weight on his chest was forcing the air from his lungs. He didn't have the strength to throw the man off again.

"Perhaps I'll just strangle you," Professor Gordon decided. "I think that will be easiest." His hands closed around Bruce's throat before he had even finished speaking, digging deep into the unprotected flesh. "Hurts, doesn't it?"

It did hurt, but Bruce barely felt the pain through his panic. He couldn't breathe. He was going to black out. And if he did, he knew he'd never wake up again. He brought his own hands up and grabbed the professor's, struggling to loosen their grip, but the professor held on easily, laughing at Bruce's feeble efforts. "Bye-bye, Mr. Patman," he said, choking down harder. "See you at the movies."

Professor Gordon's demented eyes bore down into Bruce's. There was no more air. No more office around him. No more professor. Only the eyes remained—hateful, mocking eyes. Bruce stopped struggling and let his hands fall to his sides. This was it—the end.

But those horrible eyes . . .

Wincing, Bruce brought up his right hand again, hesitated, then jabbed it forward viciously, his fingers poking into damp, soft flesh.

"Ahh!" the professor screamed, releasing Bruce's throat to grab at his injured face. "My eyes!"

Triumphant, Bruce struggled out from underneath his killer. He had to get out of there while Professor Gordon was sprawled on the floor, still covering his eyes. But he had to grab the Scotch first.

He tottered toward the desk, barely able to stay on his feet. His hand reached for the decanter shakily. Suddenly a fierce, unexpected pain shot through his body, and Bruce dropped to his knees, doubling over and curling into a fetal position.

"I can still see well enough to throw a punch, you know," Professor Gordon mocked, his strong hand burying itself in Bruce's thick hair. Bruce's head was jerked backward, bringing him down to the floor. Before Bruce could react, the professor grabbed the electrical cord of a nearby floor lamp and violently yanked the plug free of the wall. A split second later the cord was around Bruce's neck, cutting into his flesh.

Bruce gagged and choked, grabbing desperately at the cord. He couldn't loosen it. His feet kicked wildly, reflexively, as the life seeped from his body.

"Oh, this works much better than fingers," he heard Professor Gordon say through a fog.

It was over. *Good-bye, Lila,* Bruce thought. *I love you. Good-bye, Mom and Dad.* The thought of never seeing any of them again brought tears to his eyes. They ran uncontrolled down his cheeks as Bruce gasped for the last precious seconds of his life.

So this was how it ended. The guy who'd always had everything was about to lose it all. *I never even appreciated it,* Bruce realized with overwhelming sadness. *I had it all, and I never appreciated any of it.*

The blackness closed in, and Bruce's body went gradually limp. Maybe five more seconds of consciousness. Maybe less. *If I get another chance,* he vowed, *I'll never forget for a second how precious life really is.*

Chapter Fifteen

I know Professor Gordon's office is right along here somewhere, Jessica thought as she sped around the final corner of the hallway on Professor Gordon's floor. Her footsteps rang out, echoing in the empty corridor. *Aha!* she cheered silently, spotting his door and reaching for the knob, praying it would be unlocked. It was. *Now it's time for some heavy snooping action.* Without hesitation Jessica threw open the door and stepped inside. What she found was so awful and unexpected that she froze on the spot, horrified.

Bruce was lying on his back on the floor and Professor Gordon was kneeling over him, choking him with a lamp cord. The professor's face was an angry, purplish red. Bruce wasn't moving. Professor Gordon looked so psychotic, so fiercely intent, it was obvious he hadn't even heard Jessica come in.

Jessica opened her mouth to scream, but all that came out was a breathy squeak. *There's no one around to hear me anyway,* she suddenly realized. *And if I keep my mouth shut, maybe I won't even be seen.* It was all up to her now.

Gulping at the weight of her responsibility, Jessica searched the room for something to hit Professor Gordon with. She almost immediately spotted a large liquor decanter near the edge of the desk. It looked heavy enough.

In a flash she ran to the desk, grabbed the decanter by the neck, and wound up once before bringing it down hard on the professor's head, her strength matched by the intensity of her fear. The decanter exploded into shards, spraying crystal and liquor everywhere. Professor Gordon slumped to the floor, unconscious.

"Bruce!" Jessica cried, dropping to her knees and unwrapping the electrical cord from around his neck. "Bruce, can you hear me?"

Bruce's head lolled back and forth on the rug.

"You're still alive!" Jessica cried, wrapping her arms around him in a big hug before she could stop herself.

"Oof," Bruce gasped. "Jessica—stop—I need air."

Jessica let him go. "Sorry," she breathed as Bruce's hands rose slowly to touch the ugly red welts on his throat. "You saved my life," Bruce croaked gratefully, his unfocused eyes struggling to hold Jessica's. "How?"

Jessica glanced nervously at the conked-out professor before she picked up one of the larger pieces of broken crystal to show to Bruce. "I hit him with this. It was a big old liquor bottle."

"What!"

Bruce rolled onto his stomach and managed to get up on his hands and knees. Once he was there, however, the room seemed to tilt in front of him and he swayed first left, then right, trying to level the horizon. Every part of his body ached, especially his neck, and the pounding in his ears was so loud that he could barely hear anything else.

He still couldn't believe the irony of what had happened. Jessica had saved his life, all right. And then she had killed him again.

The decanter had been shattered into what seemed like a million pieces. All the precious Scotch had disappeared, wicked down into the thick oriental carpet. It was truly over. There was nothing left for the doctors to analyze.

Bruce managed to steady himself long enough to look around the room. Jessica was on the telephone, calling the police. Professor Gordon lay on the floor, completely unconscious, a small rivulet of blood trickling out of his hair and over his forehead. *Jessica really let him have it,* Bruce realized, awed, but the knowledge brought him no pleasure. If the professor had been conscious, Bruce might at least have had one last chance to find out the name of the poison.

Bruce's eyes traveled to the window, which was growing steadily lighter behind the crimson drapes. With an effort Bruce crawled to it and pulled the draperies open, wanting to see the dawn. His last dawn.

The fabric gave beneath his fingers, and Bruce pulled himself up to his feet, using the windowsill for support. He was finally standing, the SVU campus spread out before him in the early morning light. He'd done everything he could to save his own life, but now his time was up.

How will it happen? he wondered. *Will I just gradually fade away, or will I have some type of sudden attack? Will it hurt?* The thoughts in his head didn't seem like his own as he stood there watching the beginnings of his final sunrise.

"Bruce, come on," Jessica called from behind him. "Help me tie Professor Gordon up until the police get here."

Reluctantly Bruce took his eyes off the peaceful scene below him, turning to help Jessica. As he did, a shiny object in the very corner of the windowsill caught his attention.

"What's that?" he muttered, turning back to the window and struggling with the heavy drape. He finally pulled it aside, revealing a cut-crystal glass sparkling in the first low rays of daylight.

There sat his Scotch glass from Wednesday,

still partially full. Either he was imagining things, or Professor Gordon had never found it.

Carefully, shakily Bruce reached out to it as if it were a mirage—the final delusion of a dying man. But instead of disappearing as he touched it, the glass remained solid in his grip. Bruce lifted it tenderly from the sill, cradling it in both hands.

A new burst of life shot through him, carried on a wave of hope. "Jessica, look!" he shouted. His voice came out a whisper. "This—this is what he poisoned me with. We have to get this to Dr. Martin."

Jessica looked up from where she was kneeling on the floor, tying the professor's hands behind him with the same lamp cord he'd used to strangle Bruce. Her eyes widened in amazement. "Unbelievable!" she said. "Now hang on a second while I tie his feet."

"Forget it, Jessica. There's no time. Let's go!" Bruce urged impatiently, still cupping the Scotch glass with both hands.

Jessica stood and took one last look down at Professor Gordon before she turned to Bruce. "Let me carry that," she said, reaching for his treasure.

"No!" he exclaimed, snatching it away from her. Then more calmly, "I can do it."

"You're sick," Jessica argued. "You might drop it."

"My life is in this glass," Bruce said solemnly. "I'm not going to drop it."

      °   °   °

"Well, you're looking much better," the nurse said cheerily, dropping Lila's wrist and noting her pulse on the chart. "You'll be out of here by noon, I'll bet."

Noon. Everything she saw, everything she heard only reminded Lila that Bruce's time was running out. Lila had never noticed before how many clocks were in the world, but now they were everywhere she looked. Without even moving her head she could see one on the nurse's wrist, one on the wall by the television, and another one out in the hall.

"I want to get up," Lila announced.

"Get up?" the nurse repeated, surprised. "What for?"

"I want to see Dr. Martin."

"You don't need to see a doctor, hon," the nurse said reassuringly. "You're fine."

Lila nodded, her lips tight. No point wasting time arguing. She'd simply wait for the woman to leave the room, then get up and find Dr. Martin herself.

As soon as the nurse stepped into the hall and closed the door behind her, Lila threw back the covers and slipped out of bed. Her head still ached enormously, but the drugs they'd given her for pain had taken the edge off, making the throbbing bearable. She had a concussion, but she'd live. There was no reason she couldn't try to help Bruce.

Lila found her clothes in the closet and put them on. The understated, formal outfit she'd worn to Andre's the evening before looked garish and out of place in the harsh lighting of the hospital, and her high heels were hardly meant for sneaking around. After a moment's hesitation Lila pulled the hospital gown on over her clothes like a coat, put on the hospital-issued slippers, and crept to her door. She opened it cautiously. No one was in the hall.

Lila sidled down the hallway toward the elevator, expecting to be stopped at any second, but no one appeared. She reached the elevator, stepped inside and pressed *L*, then slumped against the chrome railing along one wall, gripping it hard for support. She wasn't quite as strong as she'd thought.

The doors chimed open on the first floor, and Lila stepped uneasily out into the lobby. A sign directly across from the elevator listed the various departments on the floor, with arrows indicating their directions. Lila turned left for the laboratory.

"Can I help you?" asked a pleasant-looking male desk attendant as Lila pushed through the swinging door into the lab.

"I . . . I'd like to see Dr. Martin," Lila stuttered, prepared to insist if necessary.

"Sure. She's right back there. First door on the left."

Lila walked uncertainly past the desk and hesitated outside the door the young man had indicated.

"Go on in," he urged. "She won't mind."

Inside the room was a counter that ran along three walls, with white cupboards filling the spaces above and below it. The doctor sat hunched on a stool with her back to the door, performing a complicated-looking test. She continued with her chemicals and eyedroppers, apparently unaware of Lila's presence, and Lila waited silently, not wanting to distract her.

"OK," the doctor muttered under her breath. "Here we go." Using yet another eyedropper, she carefully placed a small amount of a pink solution into a test tube containing a clear liquid. Nothing happened. "No!" the doctor exclaimed, pushing the failed test away impatiently. She dropped her head into her hands momentarily but in the next second drew a deep breath and raised it again, pulling the testing equipment back into position in front of her.

"Excuse me, Dr. Martin?" Lila said softly. "I'm Lila Fowler, Bruce Patman's girlfriend."

Dr. Martin spun around on her stool immediately. "Where's Bruce?" she asked, an urgent tone in her voice. "Is he here? Have you heard from him?"

Lila shook her head. "Have you found the antidote yet?" she asked, knowing she'd already witnessed the answer.

"No," Dr. Martin groaned. She looked exhausted, and Lila suddenly realized that she must have been awake and working for nearly twenty-four hours. "I'm so close. I really thought that last test . . ." She sighed. "We'll just have to keep trying. Have a seat if you like."

The doctor gestured at a small rolling chair near the door before returning to her test tubes, and Lila sank into it gratefully. At least she knew what was happening now, even if the news wasn't what she'd hoped.

Lila squeezed her eyelids shut against the tears that burned there. *I'd give anything to see him one last time,* she thought, trying to suppress her sobs. *Even if there was no hope left, at least we'd have a few moments together before—* She cringed, cutting off her thought.

A large wall clock mounted directly over the doctor's head seemed to stare Lila down, but she no longer needed a clock to count the time being lost. Her own heart beat out the seconds, the minutes. Her pulse was a merciless countdown.

A loud noise from the room outside the doctor's laboratory made Lila jolt up in the chair. And then came the sound Lila feared she'd never hear again—Bruce's voice.

"Where's Dr. Martin?" he asked weakly.

"This way!" Lila heard Jessica answer. "Come on!"

"Bruce!" Lila exclaimed, jumping up. She had

barely managed to stand before the door crashed open and a haggard, bruised Bruce and a frantic Jessica rushed into the lab.

"We've got the poison!" Jessica exclaimed, dashing past Lila as if she hadn't noticed her. "Dr. Martin, we've got it!"

Bruce staggered toward the doctor, a crystal glass with an inch or so of brownish liquid in his hand. "It's in this Scotch," he said, handing it over.

The doctor took the glass and stared down into it for a second before she glanced up at the clock. She turned to Bruce and appeared somewhat startled by his appearance. She quickly gathered herself together to examine his eyes and feel the pulse in his neck. A smile slowly spread across her face. "I think we're going to make it," she said.

"Bruce!" Lila cried, rushing forward. "Oh, Bruce!"

"Lila?" He turned slowly, his face working with emotion as their eyes connected. Before she could stop herself, Lila was sobbing—this time with joy.

"Oh, Bruce, you're going to live!" she cried, throwing her arms around him and burying her face against his chest. He smelled awful, but Lila didn't care. She clung to him for all she was worth. "You're going to live," she repeated, lifting her head to see his beautiful, unfocused eyes.

Bruce just smiled—a slow, puzzled, wonderful smile. "I am," he said dazedly. Then he slid out of her arms and onto the floor.

"Bruce!" Lila shrieked.

"Sorry," he murmured against the linoleum. "A little weak . . ."

"Oh no!" Dr. Martin stepped over him and pushed the door open. "Peter!" she called loudly to the attendant outside. "Get Mr. Patman into a bed. Stat!"

Chapter
Sixteen

"Where's Dr. Martin? What's taking so long?" Lila wondered anxiously, pacing back and forth at the foot of Bruce's hospital bed.

"You want me to go check on her?" Jessica offered eagerly, jumping up out of her chair.

"Yes!" Lila said.

"No," Bruce croaked. "Leave her alone. She'll be here as soon as she can."

"But Bruce . . . ," Lila began.

"Let her be." The effort of speaking was almost too great, especially since his throat was bruised and sore where the professor had choked him, but Bruce didn't want the doctor to be distracted. He knew that Lila and Jessica were trying to help, but at this point they'd only get in the doctor's way. With every technician in the lab working on that Scotch, isolating the poison couldn't take much longer. It had to happen—and soon. After everything he'd been through, it would be too cruel if he died.

Still, he was so weak that he could barely hold on, even though vital fluids and painkillers were being dripped into his veins through an IV. The painkillers quelled his agony only slightly; they seemed to affect his consciousness more. Bruce struggled to keep his eyes open, knowing he had only minutes left.

"How are you feeling?" Lila whispered, coming to his bedside and taking his hand. "Better?" There was a long pause when Bruce didn't answer. "Worse?"

"Not great," Bruce admitted at last. Lila's face contorted with fear. "Don't worry—she'll be here soon." He desperately hoped he was right.

The door swung open at that very moment, and Dr. Martin strode into the room. "I think I've got it," she said quickly, holding up a syringe of yellow liquid. She crossed to Bruce's bed and injected the antidote through a port in Bruce's IV, enabling it to seep slowly into his bloodstream from a vein in the back of his hand. "How's that?" she asked.

"I . . . I don't really feel anything," Bruce said worriedly. "Maybe a little burning where it's going into my hand."

"That's perfectly normal," Dr. Martin replied. She watched Bruce carefully as the antidote coursed through his body, monitoring his vital signs. The clouds across his eyes seemed to clear slightly as Bruce watched the doctor anxiously for some type of sign.

"My sight's clearing up a little," Bruce offered. "But maybe that's just wishful thinking."

Five agonizing minutes passed. Then ten. Bruce watched them tick by on the clock. He wasn't afraid anymore. He'd accept his fate either way.

He watched Lila worrying the hem of her dress and Jessica gnawing at her cuticles. He watched Dr. Martin take notes. And he watched the clock. Fifteen minutes. Then twenty. He was still alive.

"Well, I think you're very lucky," Dr. Martin said after a half hour had passed. "I believe you're going to make it."

Lila and Jessica gasped with happy relief, and Lila rushed to his side.

"Luck had nothing to do with it," Bruce grumbled, trying to keep from smiling. "You wouldn't believe what I've been through in the last twenty-four hours."

The doctor laughed. "It hasn't exactly been a Hawaiian vacation around here either," she reminded him. "Even so, you must realize how easily you could have died, how very close you came. You've been given a second chance—I hope you appreciate it."

The doctor's words triggered a memory so

strong that Bruce saw the scene before his eyes almost as clearly as if he were reliving it: Professor Gordon had him down on his back again; he was about to pass out. *I had it all, and I never appreciated any of it,* he'd thought. *If I get another chance, I'll never forget for a second how precious life really is.* He remembered it all vividly.

Bruce shook his head to clear the scene. As he did he suddenly realized that the ringing in his ears was much quieter than before. His breathing was coming more easily too. And daylight was streaming in through the window blinds.

"I think I'll appreciate it," he told Dr. Martin, closing his eyes. "I think I'll appreciate it every single day."

Lila sat at the edge of Bruce's bed, watching him. He'd been asleep for hours, but a nurse came in to check on him every so often and to reassure Lila that he was doing fine. Jessica had gone home to shower and get some sleep herself, but Lila wasn't tired. The lump on her head was already less swollen, and all she could think about was how lucky she was to have Bruce back.

She had to smile when she remembered how furious she'd been with him only the day before, when she'd found him in bed in Jessica's room. Jessica had explained everything beautifully, of course, and they'd had a huge laugh over it. It was behind them now. *All* the bad times were behind them now.

The hospital-room door opened a crack, and the nurse stuck her head inside. "Lila!" she whispered, motioning for Lila to come out into the hall. With a last, lingering look at Bruce, Lila got up.

"What's going on?" she asked curiously as soon as she'd closed Bruce's door behind her. There was a tall woman with the nurse who Lila had never seen before.

"I'm Detective Finley," the woman said. "We spoke on the phone."

"Yes, of course."

"Can we talk somewhere in private for a few minutes?"

"Sure."

Lila followed Detective Finley into a vacant room. Taking a seat on the edge of the empty bed, the detective motioned Lila into a chair.

"We caught Dennis Gordon," Detective Finley said immediately. "He admits to attacking you."

Lila gasped with relief. She'd been so worried about Bruce, she hadn't realized until that moment how frightened she'd been that the professor would somehow talk his way out of the whole thing. "It wasn't just me," Lila said, eager to tell the detective everything she'd discovered. "He poisoned Bruce too."

The detective nodded. "We know. I'm afraid Mr. Gordon was pretty busy last night. He also shot and killed another of his students—a man named Marcus Stanton."

"No!" Lila's hand flew to her mouth, the shock making her nauseous. Tears started down her cheeks. "Oh no," she whispered softly.

"You knew him?" the detective asked, surprised.

Lila nodded. "Not very well. We . . . we went out once."

The detective produced a little notepad and wrote something down. "Well, that's a connection I have to admit we weren't aware of," she said. "I'm sorry if the way I broke the news upset you."

Lila shook her head, and more tears spilled down her cheeks. She couldn't believe that Marcus was dead. She'd suspected him of being dangerous, but he'd actually been in danger himself. Maybe that was why he'd lied to her.

"I didn't know him well," Lila repeated, "but there were a couple of things Marcus said that bothered me. I don't know if they're important."

"Like what?" asked Detective Finley, very interested.

"Well, he lied about the school he went to—he told me he went to Hillhaven and was on their tennis team. He lied about knowing a friend of mine. I . . . I got the feeling he lied about a lot of things."

"I'm not surprised," the detective replied. "If Professor Gordon can be believed at all, Marcus managed to steal all Belinda Beringer's money right out of her trust fund. He had a lot to hide."

"Belinda Beringer?" Lila repeated, confused.

"You didn't know that either? Marcus was Belinda's fiancé—you do know who Belinda Beringer is, don't you?"

"Of course," Lila managed. "She's the film student who committed suicide."

"She also went to Hillhaven," Detective Finley offered. "Perhaps that made it easier for him to lie about it."

And maybe that's how he got the T-shirt, Lila realized. Then a horrible thought occurred to her. "You don't think Marcus . . ." She couldn't even finish the sentence. The thought of having been out with him, of having been *alone* with him, made her shudder.

"No, we don't," the detective said matter-of-factly, interrupting Lila's thoughts. "Several elements of Bruce's case make us pretty confident that Dennis Gordon is responsible for Belinda's death too, although he hasn't admitted it. We're reopening her case, and we're hoping Bruce will have some information that can help us. We have reason to believe he was on the scene when Marcus was murdered."

"He was?" Lila said weakly. Obviously she and Bruce had a lot of catching up to do.

The detective smiled. "He wouldn't give the operator his name, but we have his voice on a nine-one-one tape. Lucky for him, Professor Gordon already confessed. Otherwise Bruce would be our prime suspect."

"You're not serious!" Lila gasped.

"I'm afraid so." The detective nodded. "Especially now that I know you dated Marcus."

Lila took in the information quietly, in a state of disbelief. *Imagine what could have happened if the police* hadn't *believed Bruce was innocent!* she thought, knowing his prison sentence would have been all her fault. No matter what happened, she'd never scheme to make him jealous again.

"Well, I just wanted to let you know that we're on top of your case," Detective Finley said. "We'll have more questions for you later, and eventually you'll have to testify, but it looks like things are under control for now."

"Thanks," Lila said gratefully.

"No problem." Detective Finley rose to her feet. "Would you let Bruce know that we want to talk to him the minute he's feeling up to it?"

Lila nodded. "Sure."

The detective left the room, and Lila sat alone for a few minutes before she got up and walked back into the hall. Quietly Lila let herself back into Bruce's room and slipped into her chair at his bedside. His breathing was even and regular, and the color was coming back into his cheeks. She took his hand and squeezed it hard, unable to stop herself.

Bruce's eyes fluttered open and roamed the room a moment before locking on Lila's.

"Li," he whispered, squeezing her hand in return. "It's good to see you."

"It's good to see *you*," she returned, suddenly overwhelmed by tears again. She buried her face in the blankets at Bruce's side, weeping.

Bruce removed his hand from hers and gently stroked her hair. "Don't worry, Lila," he murmured soothingly. "I promise I'll never work so hard on my homework again."

"I'm back, and I've got pizza!" Jessica announced as she let herself into Bruce's room.

"All right, dinnertime!" Bruce boomed. He was sitting up in bed, looking like a new man. His hair was brushed, his face had been shaved, and there was even a self-satisfied glow in his eyes again. Lila, on the other hand, looked pale and exhausted.

"I brought *you* some more comfortable clothes," Jessica added, tossing a small overnight bag to Lila.

"Way to go, Jessica," Bruce said approvingly, pulling his bedside tray into position over his lap. "Just put the pizza right here."

Jessica dropped the hot, greasy cardboard box onto the tray and fished a cold six-pack of sodas out of her tote bag, along with some paper plates and napkins.

"Thanks. You thought of everything," Lila said gratefully, holding up the soft, pink Theta Alpha Theta sweatshirt Jessica had brought her.

"I know," Jessica said, pleased with herself. "I'm a genius."

"How about handing me a plate, genius?" Bruce teased. "You wouldn't believe the slop they try to pass off as dinner in here."

Jessica dropped comfortably onto the end of Bruce's bed and passed out plates, sodas, and napkins three ways. Lila managed to convince Bruce to part with a couple of slices of "his" pizza, and soon they were all eating ravenously.

"This is so *good*," Lila managed between bites. "I don't even remember when I last ate."

"You can't call that congealed pudding substitute they brought me for dinner *eating*," Bruce added, taking another huge bite of the pepperoni-laden pizza.

Jessica smiled as she chewed her slice. Judging by his attitude, Bruce was already almost back to normal.

"Hey! Has anyone seen the news?" Jessica asked suddenly. "I wonder if we're on it."

"Oh! Turn it on," Lila urged.

Bruce hit the remote on the side of his bed, and the television sprang to life. He flipped through the channels and stopped on a local news broadcast before going back to his pizza. The anchorwoman was doing a story about a litter of wild kittens someone had discovered under their deck.

"Oh, well," Jessica said discontentedly. "I can see how murder and a celebrity arrest could get lost in the excitement of a litter of kittens."

"Maybe we already missed it," Lila suggested, setting down her empty plate. "I'm going to go put on those clothes you brought me." She rose and walked into Bruce's little bathroom with her overnight bag, shutting the door behind her.

"More," Jessica demanded, holding her own empty plate in Bruce's direction. "Give it up."

Bruce filled her plate with another huge slice of pizza. "So much for the diet," he teased.

"Oh, please," Jessica responded. "I think I worked it off on the Bruce Patman exercise program from hell."

"You know you dug it," he countered. "If it wasn't for me, you'd have spent the whole night sitting home without a date again."

"That's what you think!" Jessica retorted. "And by the way, you owe me a new dress and a pair of sandals, Mr. Back-from-the-Dead."

She glared at him across the length of the hospital bed, her angry blue-green eyes boring into his, and he returned her gaze. They had only held the stare-down for maybe five seconds, though, before the corners of Bruce's mouth started to twitch, then to turn up. Jessica saw the movement and, to her dismay, felt her own traitorous mouth curve

271

into a smile. A moment later they were both laughing out loud.

"What's going on out here?" Lila asked, stepping back into the room wearing the sweatshirt with a pair of jeans.

Jessica, still giggling, had opened her mouth to explain when Bruce suddenly pointed to the television set. "Look!" The face of an overserious anchorman filled the screen.

"And to recap our top story of the day," the man droned over a close-up of Professor Gordon being put into a police car, "Dennis Gordon, Academy Award–winning screenwriter and Sweet Valley University professor, was arrested early this morning on charges of attempted murder. The charges were amended to murder and two counts of attempted murder later in the day. More charges are expected to follow as more information is uncovered."

"Oh, more charges will follow," Bruce predicted confidently. "They don't know the half of it yet."

"That reminds me," Jessica said. "Did you turn in that stolen car?"

"There's a stolen car?" Lila exclaimed, appalled.

"Well, yeah, Li," Bruce admitted reluctantly, shooting Jessica a dirty look. "We needed something to drive in after Jessica sailed the Porsche off the top of that cliff."

Lila turned to face Jessica. "You did *what?*" she said weakly, reaching for her chair.

"It was dark!" Jessica defended herself. "And we were only going about a hundred miles an hour. Bruce couldn't have done any better."

"So where's the Porsche now?" Lila asked.

Jessica made a face and looked timidly at Bruce.

"In the bottom of a canyon in Crestview," he said. "Either that or some brave person has already pulled it out for scrap."

"Scrap," Lila repeated softly. "Does this story never end?"

Bruce smiled. "It's a hell of a ride, isn't it?" he said proudly. "I knew that when I wrote it."

Chapter Seventeen

"Oh, cool!" Bruce exclaimed, waving the express delivery courier into his enormous, private hospital suite. "Are those my Porsche brochures?"

"I don't know, sir," the young man answered. "Are you Bruce Patman?" He walked hesitantly into the room, seemingly distracted by the unusually large number of elaborate flower arrangements.

Bruce nodded impatiently. "Yeah, that's me."

"I need you to sign here, then," the courier said, approaching the bed and passing Bruce an electronic pad. Bruce scrawled his name hastily and ripped into the thick envelope before the courier was even all the way out of the room. A glossy Porsche brochure with an accompanying CD-ROM disk spilled out onto the blankets.

"This is so suave," Bruce breathed, grabbing the brochure and eagerly inspecting the full-color photograph on the front. "I can't wait to get out of here and buy one!"

"Well, you won't have to wait much longer." Dr. Martin laughed, walking in through the open door. "I'm discharging you tomorrow."

"Excellent! I mean, no offense, but a week in this place is plenty."

"None taken." The doctor grinned. "I know what you mean."

Dr. Martin looked at the chart at the foot of the bed and examined Bruce's throat. "The poison is completely out of your system," she reported, "and there are no signs of any lasting effects. Your neck looks pretty bad, but it's all just bruising and superficial abrasions. They'll fade soon."

"They're not going to start fading today, I hope!" Bruce said worriedly.

Dr. Martin looked at him strangely, but before she could respond, there was a commotion at the door.

"Hi! How's the invalid?" came Jessica's cheery voice from behind the doctor.

"I made you some cookies, Bruce," Lila added proudly, stepping up to the bedside. "I baked them all by myself."

Lila baking? Bruce thought, alarmed at the thought of his rich, sheltered girlfriend attempting anything by herself in the kitchen. But then he smiled. After all, what were the odds of being poisoned twice in one week? "Great!" he said, patting the bed at his side for Lila to sit down. "Bring them on!"

Dr. Martin said her good-byes, and the two girls took seats—Lila on the bed and Jessica in the chair beside it. "Try one," Lila said, handing Bruce a misshapen lump of a cookie. "They're chocolate chip."

Bruce had just bitten into the dry, crumbly cookie when the phone next to his bed rang. "Hello?" he managed, trying hard to swallow the cookie dust in his mouth.

"Bruce!" gushed a woman's voice on the other end. "This is Sylvia Henning. Remember me?"

"Vaguely," Bruce said, amused. He pointed at the receiver and mouthed, "Agent," to Lila and Jessica.

"Another one?" Lila complained loudly.

"What can I do for you, Sylvia?" Bruce asked, ignoring Lila's interruption. Bruce was far from sharing Lila's disgust with the Hollywood feeding frenzy over his script; in fact, he was enjoying every minute of it.

"I want to know if you've selected an agent yet," Sylvia said bluntly. "Just *everyone* wants to represent *The Victim*, I know that, but here at Henning Unlimited we can negotiate a deal for that screenplay that will surpass your wildest dreams."

"I don't know," Bruce said. "My dreams are pretty wild."

Sylvia laughed. "Darling, aren't everyone's? What would you say if I told you I have standing bids of over a million dollars from two different studios? That's right now, as we speak."

Bruce's eyebrows shot up. "Over a million? But you don't even have the script!"

"Not yet," Sylvia said smoothly. "I'm not going to lie to you, Bruce. *Anyone* could sell this script. Now that Dennis Gordon has confessed to killing Belinda Beringer and trying to steal *The Victim* for his follow-up project, you could probably sell it yourself. But *I'll* get top dollar for it. I'll get you control over every detail. I'll get you things you don't even know you want yet."

"I know I want a new Porsche," Bruce ventured.

Sylvia laughed again. "That's nothing! I can get that thrown in as a bonus. We're talking national news interest *and* potential Academy Award material here, Bruce. So do we have a deal?"

Bruce hesitated only a second. "Why don't you come on over? We can talk about the details in person."

"I'll be right down!" Sylvia agreed excitedly. "You won't regret this. By the way, can I bring you anything?"

"Yeah. How about a pizza?" Bruce glanced over at Lila's bone-dry cookies, knowing he'd have to eat every one. "And some milk."

"Oh, Bruce," Sylvia said with another laugh.

"I'm going to teach you to think much, much bigger!"

"Well, it looks like I've got an agent," Bruce said, hanging up the phone. "By the way, Lila, did you hire that photographer I wanted?"

"Yes, but I still don't understand why you want someone to take your picture with your neck looking that way," she objected. "The police already took photos for evidence."

"And these are for publicity," Bruce said with a smile. "Once I leak these photos to the press, the bidding war for *The Victim* ought to really heat up."

"Bruce Patman, you haven't changed a bit," Jessica exclaimed. She gestured to the Porsche brochure on his bed and to the floral arrangements and fruit baskets sent by would-be agents. "You almost died, and still all you think about is money and cars and . . . and getting your picture taken!"

"That's not true!" Bruce protested. "Lila, that's not what *you* think, is it?"

"I don't know, Bruce," Lila said, averting her eyes. "You do seem awfully caught up in all this. . . ."

"It's a game!" he said quickly, taking her hand. "It's only a game—I know it isn't real."

"And what do you think *is* real?" Lila challenged.

"You are," Bruce answered sincerely. "And me with you—the two of us together. Our friends, our families. That's all I really care about."

"Well . . ."

"I promise you, Lila, from now on I'm going to appreciate my life—and everyone in it—a whole lot more."

Tears of joy sparkled in Lila's eyes. "Do you mean that?" she whispered.

"Absolutely," Bruce said, sinking back into his pillows, a satisfied smile on his face. Of course he meant it. After all, life was great. *If they make my movie this year,* he wondered, *will it be eligible for the next Academy Awards? Or will I have to wait until the ceremony after that?*

"Which designer would you want to make your dress for the Academy Awards?" Bruce asked his girlfriend suddenly, snapping out of his reverie. "You ought to pick someone soon."

"I'm sure!" Jessica protested. "It's just like you to assume you'll even be invited, Bruce."

But Lila's eyes shone with excitement. "Do you mean it?" she breathed. "Do you really think we're going?"

Bruce reached out to her and folded her into his arms, his heart overflowing with happiness. "Buy a dress, Li," he urged softly. "And be sure to go all out. I want everyone there to see me with the most beautiful woman alive."

"Well, I'll be proud to be with the most handsome man alive," Lila replied, emphasizing the word *alive*.

Created by Francine Pascal

The *valley* has never been so *sweet*!

Having left Sweet Valley High School behind them, Jessica and Elizabeth Wakefield have begun a new stage in their lives, attending the most popular university around – Sweet Valley University!

Join them and all their friends for fun, frolics and frights on *and* off campus.

Ask your bookseller for any titles you may have missed. The Sweet Valley University series is published by Bantam Books.